UNTIL FRIDAY NIGHT

UNTIL FRIDAY NIGHT

A Field Party Novel

BY
ABBI GLINES

Simon Pulse

NEW YORK   LONDON   TORONTO   SYDNEY   NEW DELHI

SIMON PULSE
An imprint of Simon & Schuster Children's Publishing Division
1230 Avenue of the Americas, New York, New York 10020
First Simon Pulse hardcover edition August 2015
Text copyright © 2015 by Abbi Glines
Jacket photograph of field copyright © 2015 by Matt Erikson
Jacket photographs of truck and fence copyright © 2015 by iStockphoto
Jacket photographs of cliff, sky, teens, and lens flares copyright © 2015
by Thinkstock
SIMON PULSE and colophon are registered trademarks of
Simon & Schuster, Inc.
For information about special discounts for bulk purchases, please
contact Simon & Schuster Special Sales at 1-866-506-1949 or
business@simonandschuster.com.
The Simon & Schuster Speakers Bureau can bring authors to your live
event. For more information or to book an event contact the
Simon & Schuster Speakers Bureau at 1-866-248-3049
or visit our website at www.simonspeakers.com.
Jacket designed by Jessica Handelman
Interior designed by Mike Rosamilia
The text of this book was set in Stempel Garamond LT.
Manufactured in the United States of America
2 4 6 8 10 9 7 5 3 1
Library of Congress Cataloging-in-Publication Data
Glines, Abbi.
Until Friday Night : A Field Party novel / by Abbi Glines.—pages cm
Summary: In the small town of Lawton, Alabama, star high school
quarterback West Ashby meets new girl Maggie Carlton, both battling
feelings of grief and sorrow.
[1. Grief—Fiction. 2. Emotional problems—Fiction.
3. Love—Fiction. 4. Football—Fiction.] I. Title.
PZ7.G4888Ul 2015
[Fic]—dc23
2015010704
ISBN 978-1-4814-3885-8 (hc)
ISBN 978-1-4814-3886-5 (eBook)

To Kiki Maria and her beautiful daughter, Mila.
You always said you couldn't wait to share my books with
your daughter, Kiki. This one is for both of you.
Your beautiful spirit lives on. Remember, Mila, that your
mother is always with you. She's in your heart.

Ain't She Sweet
CHAPTER 1

MAGGIE

This wasn't home. Nothing ever would be again. And besides, I didn't want a home—the word came with memories too painful to think about.

I knew my aunt Coralee and uncle Boone were watching me closely as they led me through the house. They wanted me to like it here—there was a certain hopefulness in their eyes. I didn't remember what hope felt like. It had been so long since I'd hoped for anything.

"We gave you a room upstairs. I painted it a pretty cotton-candy blue," Aunt Coralee informed me cautiously. "I remembered that you liked blue."

It's true that I had liked blue a few Christmases ago.

Had even worn all blue one year. I wasn't necessarily a fan of it now, though. . . .

I followed both my aunt and uncle up the stairs. The family photos lining the wall made me turn my head back around and stare straight ahead. I'd had those once too. Photos that my mother proudly displayed on the walls of our home. But those photos had been lies. The smiles were never real.

"Here it is," Aunt Coralee announced as she stopped halfway down the hall and opened the door to a large bedroom. Other than the blue walls, everything else was white.

I liked it. If I weren't afraid of my own voice, I'd tell her thank you. Instead I put down the backpack from my shoulders then turned and hugged her. That would have to be enough.

"Well, I certainly hope you like *my room*," a deep voice drawled from the doorway.

"Brady, don't," Uncle Boone said in a stern voice.

"What? I was just being nice," he replied. "Kinda . . ."

I only remembered my cousin Brady a little. He had never played with me at family events, was always running off with one of the buddies he'd brought with him.

Now he was leaning against the doorframe of the bedroom, brown hair falling into his eyes, a smirk on his face. He didn't seem happy. Oh God, had they given me his room?

That couldn't be good. I didn't want to take his room.

"Brady's just being a brat," Aunt Coralee explained quickly. "He's perfectly happy about moving to the attic room. He's been at us for two years to fix up that space for him so he'd have somewhere more private."

A large hand landed on my shoulder as Uncle Boone came to stand beside me. "Son, you remember Maggie," he said in a voice that didn't leave room for argument.

Brady was staring at me. He looked annoyed at first, but his expression suddenly softened into something resembling concern. "Yeah, I remember her."

Uncle Boone continued, "You'll need to show her around at school on Monday. Y'all are in the same grade, and we made sure they put her in several of your classes so you could help her out." I had a feeling Brady already knew all this. The information was for me.

Brady sighed and shook his head. "Y'all don't even know," he muttered before walking off.

"I'm sorry about him," Aunt Coralee said. "He's become so moody, and we don't know what to do with him half the time."

Even if I did speak, I didn't have a response for that.

She squeezed my arm. "We're gonna let you get settled in. Unpack, and rest if you need. If you want company, I'll be in the kitchen, cooking dinner. You're welcome to go anywhere in the house you'd like. Make yourself at home."

There was that word again: *home*.

My aunt and uncle left me alone, finally, and retreated down the hall. I stood in the pretty blue room and realized, much to my surprise, that I already felt safe. I'd thought the comfort of safety was long gone for me.

"So, you really don't talk?" Brady's voice filled the room, and I spun around to see my cousin back in the doorway.

I really didn't want him to dislike me or be annoyed about my being here. But I wasn't sure how to convince him that I'd keep to myself, that I wouldn't bother him or change his life.

"Shit, this ain't gonna be easy. You're—" He paused and let out a laugh that didn't sound like he meant it. "This shit is gonna be worse than I thought. Least you could have helped me out and been ugly."

Excuse me?

Brady frowned. "Just don't draw attention to yourself. My momma finally got the daughter she never had, but it don't make shit easier for me. I have a life, you know."

I simply nodded. I was sure he had a life. He was tall with dark hair and light hazel eyes, and his wide shoulders hinted at the muscles underneath his T-shirt. No doubt girls loved him.

I had no intention of being in his way, but I could see

how my coming into his home and taking his room would make it seem otherwise. And now his parents had me in his classes, too.

But I'd prove he had nothing to worry about. I picked up my backpack again and took out the pad and pen I always kept with me.

"What're you doing?" he asked, clearly confused.

I quickly wrote:

Promise I won't be in your way. Don't expect you to help me at school. Just let your parents think you are, and I'll go along with it. Sorry I took your room. We can switch back if you want.

I handed the note pad to Brady and let him read it. When he finished, he sighed deeply and handed the pad back to me.

"You can keep the room. Mom's right. I like the attic. I was just being an ass. You think you won't need me at school, but you will. Can't be helped." And with that, he walked away.

I stood at the doorway as he made his way down to the kitchen. I started to shut the door when I heard Brady's voice travel up the stairs.

"What's for dinner?" he asked.

"Chicken spaghetti. I thought Maggie might like it since it's your favorite," Aunt Coralee replied. Then, dropping her voice a little: "I wish you'd take the time to get to know her."

"Just talked to her. She, uh, wrote to me," he replied.

"And? Ain't she sweet?" Aunt Coralee sounded so sincere.

"Sure, Mom. She's real sweet."

But Brady didn't sound very convinced.

CHAPTER 2

WEST

I was getting drunk. That was my main goal tonight.

Slamming my truck door, I headed toward the field where I could already hear the music blasting and see the bonfire lighting the darkness. This was our last Friday night before football became our lives for the next three months. Everyone would be celebrating. Couples would be hooking up in the back of pickup trucks, everyone would have a red Solo cup full of beer in their hands, and there would be at least one fight over a girl before the night was over. It was the end to our summer and the beginning of our senior year.

But I was going to need a beer or six to celebrate.

Watching my dad throw up blood as my mother wiped his forehead with pure fear in her eyes—that had been too damn much. I should have stayed home, but I couldn't bring myself to do it. Every time he got sick, the little boy inside me came out, and I hated that feeling.

I loved my dad. He'd been my hero my entire life. How the hell was I supposed to lose him?

Shaking my head, I ran my hand through my hair and pulled hard. I was ready for the football field, and next Friday night I'd be back in my pads and helmet. But I wanted to feel some pain *now*. Anything to numb the reality of my life.

My phone started vibrating, and I pulled it out of my pocket. Every time it rang and I wasn't home, terror gripped me so strongly, I felt sick. Seeing Raleigh, my girlfriend's name, was a relief. It wasn't Mom. Nothing was wrong. Dad was still safe at home.

"Hey," I said, wondering why she was calling me. She knew I was headed to the field party.

"You coming to get me?" she asked, sounding annoyed.

"Didn't ask me to come get you. I'm already at the party."

"Are you serious? I'm not coming if you don't get me, West!" She was pissed. But Raleigh was normally pissed at me about something.

"I guess I'll see you later, then. Ain't in the mood for this tonight, Ray."

Raleigh had no idea about my dad. He didn't want people knowing how sick he was. We kept our mouths shut and, since the local hospital wasn't sufficient to treat advanced colon cancer, we took him to the hospital an hour away in Nashville. Usually you couldn't keep shit like this a secret in a small town, but we did for the most part. Made it easier that my momma didn't have many friends in Lawton, never had.

As a kid I didn't get it, but now I did. My dad had been the golden boy in high school. He was Lawton's claim to fame after playing football at the University of Alabama and then going on to play for the New Orleans Saints. While my mother, she was a total princess—her father pretty much owned most of Louisiana—and my father had fallen in love with her.

But right after my dad blew out his knee, killing his career with the Saints, he found out he'd gotten his girl-friend pregnant. He married her against her family's wishes and brought her back here to Alabama. The town saw it as: He'd been their hero, and she'd stolen him from them. Seventeen years later and they still kept her at a distance. But Momma didn't seem to care. She loved my dad. He and I, we were her world. And that was it for her.

"Are you listening to me?" Raleigh's high-pitched scream snapped me out of my thoughts.

Raleigh and I were a particular kind of couple: She liked being on my arm, and I liked the way her body looked. There was no love or trust between us. We had been dating for over a year, and she was easy to keep at a distance. And right now that's all I had the time for.

"Listen, Ray, I'm getting a headache. I need a break. Let's take a break, and we'll talk about it next week, yeah?" I didn't wait for her to respond, and hung up. I already knew it would be yelling and threats about how she'd go sleep with one of my friends. I'd heard it all before.

I just didn't care.

I picked up the pace and headed across the grass and between the trees to the open field where the parties always took place. The field belonged to Ryker and Nash Lee's grandfather. They were cousins and both played on the team. Their grandfather had been letting people use this field for parties since his sons had been in high school. It was just on the outskirts of the town limits, and their grandfather's house was the closest thing to us. And even that was a good mile away. We could make plenty of noise and not worry about nosy neighbors watching our every move.

I scanned the field and found Brady Higgens, my best friend since elementary school. He'd been passing me the football since we were in Pop Warner. Best quarterback in the state and he knew it.

Brady held up a beer in greeting when he saw me coming toward him. He was sitting on the tailgate of his truck, which he'd driven up here so we could use the generator in the back to play music. Ivy Hollis was tucked between Brady's legs. No surprise. They'd been together a lot this summer. Ivy was a senior and head cheerleader and determined to claim Brady now that his ex-girlfriend had graduated and moved halfway across the country.

"'Bout time you showed up," Brady said with a smirk, tossing me a can of beer. He rarely drank. It wasn't that he was against it, but he was determined to play at the University of Alabama next year. I had been too—once. Now I was just making it day to day, praying to God my dad didn't leave us.

Beer had become a crutch for me at these field parties. The anxiety from home was all over me, and I knew it. I needed to numb my mind.

I'm pretty sure Brady figured something was up and wanted me to tell him. Of all the women in town, his momma was the only one who was ever nice to my mother. She'd invited us to dinner many times over the years. She brought us red velvet cake during the holidays and always stopped and spoke to my mother at the games. I wondered if my mother had confided in Coralee.

"Where's Raleigh?" Ivy asked.

I ignored her. Just because she was with Brady didn't mean I had to answer her nosy-ass questions. I turned my attention to Gunner Lawton. Yeah, same damn name as the town's. The guy's great-great-great-grandfather founded it. They owned everything. He was one hell of a wide receiver, though, and around here that was what counted most.

"You alone tonight too?" I asked as I sank down on the bale of hay beside the truck.

He chuckled. "You know better. I'm just trying to decide who I want," he replied with a smirk. All Gunner had to do was crook his finger, and the girls came running. Sure, he was obnoxious about it, but when you're richer than God in a small town and one of the stars of the high school football team, you have a whole lot of power. And girls liked his looks, too.

"Let's talk football," Ryker Lee announced as he walked into our circle and sat down on the tailgate beside Brady and Ivy.

"I'd rather talk about the fact that you shaved your hair," Brady replied with a grin.

Last year Ryker had been determined to grow out his hair and get dreads. I'd been surprised to see he'd cut his hair short the first day of practice. He'd gone with his family to visit his grandmother in Georgia, so we hadn't seen him the last few weeks of summer.

"I got tired of it. I'll have dreads when I play pro. Right now I don't need that shit," he replied, and ran his hand over his head. Looked like he was gonna say something else, but then he stood up and just started staring out over the field and grinning like an idiot. "Actually, screw football. I'd rather talk about who *that* is."

I followed his gaze to see a face I didn't recognize. She was standing just on the outskirts of the party near the rows of trees. Long dark brown hair hung in soft waves over her shoulders and the prettiest green eyes I'd ever seen looked in our direction. I let my gaze move down to her mouth to see perfect unpainted pink lips.

Then there was her body. Holy hell, she made a sundress look good.

"Don't go there," Brady warned. I wanted to look at him, to read on his face why he was laying claim to the new girl when he had one tucked between his legs. But I couldn't stop looking at her. She seemed lost. And I was ready to go find her.

"Why, bro? She's hot as hell, and she looks like she needs me," Ryker replied.

"She's my cousin, dipshit," Brady snapped.

His cousin? Since when did he have a cousin?

I tore my gaze off the girl to finally look at Brady. "When did you get a cousin?"

He rolled his eyes. "You've met her. Like, years ago at one of my family Christmas things in Tennessee. She's living with us now. Just don't, okay? She's not . . . She's got some issues. She can't handle you," he said, then turned to look at Ryker and added, "or you."

"I can help with issues! I'm fucking great at that," Ryker replied, a big grin on his face.

I wasn't going to say the same thing. I had my own issues and I needed an escape, not more shit to deal with. Besides, her issues couldn't be as bad as mine. No one's could.

Brady went on. "She doesn't talk. She can't. I only brought her tonight because my momma made me. I told her she could stay with me, but she refused to. She's not all there, I don't think."

I glanced back at her, but she was gone. So, Brady had a beautiful but crazy, mute cousin. Weird.

"Shame. This year we get one new girl worth looking at and she's your cousin and a mute," Gunner said before drinking down the rest of his beer.

Brady didn't like that comment, didn't like it at all. I could see it on his face.

Gunner was right, though. We'd had the same girls in this town since elementary school. They were boring, superficial, and I'd slept with all the good-looking ones. No one was a distraction. They were all just annoying as hell.

Gunner stood up. "Going to get another beer," he announced then walked off. Gunner was our security around here. If we got caught drinking, his daddy would have enough pull with the police to get us off the hook. I actually wondered if they already knew about it and that was why they never drove out this way.

My phone started ringing again, and my stomach automatically clenched. I quickly got it out of my pocket and saw my momma's name on the screen. Shit.

Without any explanation to the guys, I just set my beer down and walked off before answering.

"Momma? Everything okay?"

"Oh yes. Just wanted you to know I left you some fried chicken in the oven to keep it warm. Also, if you could stop by the Walmart and grab some milk on your way home, that would be good."

I let out the breath I'd been holding. Dad was okay. "Sure, yeah, Momma. I'll get the milk."

"You gonna be out late?" she asked, and I noticed her voice was tense. There was something she wasn't telling me. Dad must be sick or hurting.

"I, no, uh, I'll be home soon," I assured her.

She let out a relieved sigh. "Good. Well, you drive careful. Wear your seat belt. I love you."

"Love you too, Momma."

I ended the call just as I got to where I'd parked my truck. I'd already been walking out, prepared to leave even before she'd asked if I'd be home late. It was all getting worse. Dad was hardly able to get out of bed anymore. Motherfucking doctors couldn't do anything for him.

My chest tightened, and it became hard to breathe. This had been happening more and more lately. It was like all my fears grabbed ahold of my throat and squeezed until I couldn't inhale.

Anger began to pump through my veins. This wasn't goddamn fair! My dad was a good man. He didn't deserve this. God was up there just letting this shit happen. And my sweet momma, she needed my dad. She didn't deserve this either.

"Fuck!" I roared as I slammed both hands down on the hood of my truck. This was destroying all of us, and I couldn't tell anyone. Dealing with sympathy from people who had no idea how this felt would be more shit I didn't need.

A movement from the left caught my attention, and I jerked my head to see who had witnessed my breakdown.

The sundress was the first thing I recognized. Her curvy body filled it out just perfectly.

That girl was so lucky she couldn't talk. She didn't have to pretend for anyone. She didn't have to say the right thing or act a certain way.

She tilted her head to the side as if she were studying me, deciding if I were dangerous or if I needed help. All that gorgeous hair and those full lips could certainly help. Help me forget for a moment. Forget this hell my life had become.

I shoved off of my truck and walked over to her. I almost expected her to run. She didn't.

I inhaled sharply. The tightness in my throat had eased some. "You like what you see?" I taunted her, hoping she'd run from me. She didn't deserve this; using her to ease my pain wasn't right. And I was angry and couldn't control my emotions anymore. They stayed so raw all the time. Just like everyone else in my path, she was someone I was pushing away for her own safety.

She didn't respond, but there was a clarity in her eyes. She wasn't off like Brady said—you could see that kind of thing in a person's eyes. But her eyes, they were almost too intense. Too smart.

"You just gonna stare at me like you want a taste and not speak? Kinda rude."

My own meanness made me wince inside. My momma would be ashamed of me. This girl, though, she didn't do anything more than blink. She didn't back away, and she didn't make a sound. Brady hadn't been shitting us about one thing: She really didn't talk.

But even without talking, she obviously wasn't interested in me. I wasn't used to that. Wasn't used to girls not wanting me to kiss them.

I stopped in front of her and cupped her face in one of my hands. God, that face was something else. I had to touch her to see if she was real. The perfection seemed almost impossible. Everyone had physical flaws. I wanted to find hers.

I used my thumb to brush her bottom lip. She wasn't wearing lipstick. She didn't need it—those lips were already a pretty pink.

"It's time you run along now," I warned her, even though I should have been the one to walk away.

She stayed where she was, staring up at me. Boldly. Without flinching. The only thing that gave her away was the pulse in her neck. She was nervous, but she was either too scared or too curious to move.

I took one more step until I was pressed up against her and she was backed against the tree behind her. "Told ya to run, sugar," I reminded her just before I lowered my mouth to hers.

Don't Mind Me, Sugar
CHAPTER 3

MAGGIE

I was determined not to be a hindrance to Brady. Friday night Aunt Coralee had forced him to take me to that party, and I used it as an opportunity to show him I wouldn't be a bother. Mostly, I sat in the dark by myself, away from everyone. Every thirty minutes or so I'd check if Brady was still there or looking for me, and then I'd go back to my hiding spot.

I really hoped this wasn't an every weekend event. I didn't want to have to go through that every time Brady went to the field party. I preferred to stay in my room and read. Hanging out alone in a dark field wasn't exactly my favorite way to pass the time. Although, something happened that had certainly made it less . . . boring.

Thinking of the place I'd claimed beside that tree made my cheeks flush. I'd gotten my first real kiss, and from a guy I didn't even know. He'd been so tall and his hair was dark and curled at the ends. His face . . . It was like God had taken all the perfect features for man and put them together just for this guy.

It hadn't been those things that made me stand there, though, after he warned me to go. It had been his *eyes*. Even in the darkness, I'd seen a heaviness there. A heaviness I'd never seen in anyone but myself.

He'd told his mother he loved her on the phone. Then he'd hung up and cursed while hitting his truck. Anyone who talked to his mother that way couldn't be bad. He didn't scare me.

But I was worried about him, so I stayed even when he told me to go. And then he'd kissed me. It had been rough at first, like he was trying to hurt me, but then he'd softened, and before I knew it, I was grabbing on to fistfuls of his T-shirt. My knees went weak, and I wasn't sure if I actually made a whimper or if it had just been in my head. I hoped it was in my head. Considering how abruptly he'd left me, I didn't want to have made a sound. And I wished I hadn't grabbed on to him.

It ended as suddenly as it had begun. He didn't say a word when he backed away from me. He didn't look at me. Instead he'd turned and stalked over to his truck and left. I had no idea who he was. All I knew was that he was beautiful and haunted and he'd given me a first kiss to remember.

Two hours later, when Brady had finally decided to leave, he'd found me dozing on the ground under my tree. He'd been annoyed and hadn't said anything to me on the drive home. The kiss faded into the background as I focused on how to make my cousin not hate me.

Sunday, when Brady had plans to go to a friend's house to swim, Aunt Coralee had tried to ship me off with him. But I'd written her a note telling her my period had started and I didn't feel like it, and she let me stay home.

Brady ended up being gone all day. I was sure he was worried that if he came home, she would try to foist me on him all over again.

Today I started school, and she gave Brady a to-do list all about me. I felt bad for him. You could see the frustration on his face. So I handed him a note as soon as we got there.

I got this. Do what you do, and I'll show up in class. Just cause I don't talk doesn't mean I can't get around. I'll tell Aunt Coralee you did everything she said. But I don't want you taking me everywhere. I want to do this alone.

He hadn't looked too convinced, but he nodded and took off, leaving me at the entrance of the school.

Luckily, Aunt Coralee had prepared the front office for the fact I didn't speak. They were fine with me writing down everything I needed to say. They gave me my schedule and asked where Brady was. Apparently, Aunt Coralee had also told them Brady would be my guide. I lied and wrote down that he had gone to the restroom and was meeting me in the hallway.

A small part of me—okay, a really big part of me—hoped I'd see the guy from the field party. I wanted to see him in the light. I wanted to see if he was okay. And, I hoped, maybe he'd want to see me.

Once I had directions to my locker, I went to look for it, feeling accomplished. Actually finding it was another thing entirely. With people filling the hallways, many of them in their lockers or in front of their lockers or making out against their lockers, I couldn't see the numbers. Finding 654 was basically impossible.

"You good?" Brady's voice came from behind me, and I nodded, not wanting to tell him I wasn't exactly great and would probably be late for class.

"Where's your locker?" he asked.

I thought about how to answer that and just handed him the paper with my locker number on it.

"You already passed it," he replied, nodding back down the hall. "Come on. I'll show you."

I didn't have time to write out an argument. Instead I just followed him. He was going to help me anyway and, if I admitted it to myself, I needed his help.

Unlike when *I* had walked down the hallway, fighting through the packed bodies, everyone created a path for Brady. It was like he was Moses and this was the Red Sea.

"Move the make-out fest over about five inches. Maggie can't get in her damn locker," Brady told a couple who was mid-grope-session.

"Who's Maggie?" the girl asked, turning to look at me. She had big brown eyes and an olive complexion. Her long black hair was even more striking.

"My cousin," Brady replied, sounding annoyed.

"You got a cousin?" she asked, surprised. The guy's hands, which had previously been on the girl's bottom, moved to her hips and he shifted her over. Before I could see the guy's face, Brady stepped back and held my locker open for me. "There you go. I'll be around if you need me again." Then he left me there and walked away.

I didn't make eye contact with or even look at the couple beside me. The girl giggled, then I heard the guy whisper to her—the word *mute* was something I didn't miss. Apparently, Brady had told people I was mute. I guess at least I wouldn't have anyone trying to talk to me.

"She don't talk?" the girl whispered back, loud enough for me to hear her.

I quickly put my books in my locker before closing it, making sure to hold on to my textbook and a notebook for my first class. Determined not to look at the couple, I kept my head down. My gaze landed on the guy's hands, now gripping the girl's bottom again. I guess this was something I was going to have to get used to.

I stepped into the hallway without looking up, and a hard body hit me in the side, knocking me backward.

"Shit, sorry," a male voice said as I collided with the gropey make-out couple. *Great.* "You okay?" asked the guy who ran into me.

I looked up to see a pair of the clearest blue eyes I'd ever seen, set against pretty mocha-colored skin. The combination was definitely striking but, unfortunately, he wasn't my mystery guy.

"Watch it," the girl behind me snapped, shoving me off her.

The textbook and notebook in my hands fell to the floor, causing even more of a scene. I didn't like to draw attention, but that seemed to be all I could do.

"Jesus, Raleigh, I ran into her. Chill the fuck out," the guy said as he bent down to get my books. I watched in fascination as large well-defined muscles popped from his snug short-sleeve shirt.

Raleigh laughed, but it sounded more like a wicked cackle than anything. "She's mute, Nash. And she's Brady's cousin. So you can stop with the chivalrous thing. She ain't your type."

Then, from behind me: "Don't be a bitch, babe." *That voice.* I froze. I knew that voice. No . . . don't let it be.

"Brady's got a cousin?" Nash asked as he stood up and held my books out to me.

I was afraid to turn around and look. Maybe I was mistaken. The guy making out with the girl beside me could *not* be the guy who kissed me Friday night. The guy who kissed me had been nice to his mother. Could a nice guy like that kiss another girl when he already had a girlfriend? Wasn't he a good guy deep down? I had convinced myself of that all weekend while I replayed our kiss over and over.

I tried to look unaffected as I took my books from Nash and tucked them against my chest.

"Yeah, he does. Surprise, surprise." That voice again. It *was* him. Oh God . . . it was so him.

I dropped my gaze to my books. I didn't want to look at anyone. I knew my cheeks were pink. I just wanted to be alone and get over this surprise in private.

My mystery guy continued, "She's something to look

at, but Brady's made her completely off-limits. So, Ray is
right. Let it go. I did."

But he *hadn't* stayed away. Did he know Brady had made
me off-limits when he kissed me? Was that why he was acting
now like he didn't know me at all? What a jerk! I'd let him kiss
me. What had I been thinking? I wasn't normally weak just
because a guy had a pretty face. My father had a pretty face
too, and not once had my mother been able to trust him. I was
smarter than this. That was a mistake I wouldn't make again.

"What's that supposed to mean, 'I did'?" Raleigh raised
her voice. And shoved off the guy. I moved out of her way.

"She's something to look at. Like I said," he repeated.

He was being cruel to her on purpose and using me to
do it. I hated cruelty and callous behavior. Anger simmered
inside me. It was times like this, I wanted to speak. No, I
wanted to *yell*! But I wouldn't.

My face was hot from embarrassment, fury, and disappointment. I wished Brady had waited on me. I didn't know
which way I needed to go, and pulling out my school map
in the middle of all this seemed impossible. I was trembling.
I glanced down the hall both ways, trying to decide the best
escape route.

"She's mute!" the girl yelled, then let out an angry
growl. "I don't know why I put up with you. I could have
anyone. *Anyone*, West. Do you realize that?"

West. His name was West. A girl needed to know the name of her first kiss, yet I wish I didn't. I wanted to wash him and that night from my memory completely.

"You couldn't have *me*. I don't do crazy," Nash replied, and I glanced up at him. He winked, and there was an easy friendliness in his eyes. Nothing like what I had seen in West's. Why couldn't *he* have been my first kiss?

West chuckled at Nash's reply.

"I wouldn't want you," she spit. "My daddy only lets me date white guys."

I tensed up. Had she really just said that? Nash wasn't all white, but he wasn't all black, either. He was a beautiful color.

"Awww, that's a shame," Nash replied, obviously amused. "Guess your daddy's still sore that his white girlfriend married a black man. It's been years, Raleigh. He really should move on. My momma sure has."

Okay, wow. Small towns were really, really small.

Nash looked back at me. "You need help finding your first class?" he asked.

But Raleigh wasn't about to let it die. "Are you going to allow him talk to me that way?" she asked West.

"You started it. He's just finishing it," West replied.

"I am *done*, West!" she shouted, then stormed off.

All I wanted was to get to my classroom. I reached for

the map I'd stuck in my pocket and unfolded it to figure out where I was supposed to be. Forget my trembling hands. I wanted away from this immediately. Away from West.

"What class you got first?" Nash asked me.

"She doesn't talk. Raleigh wasn't shitting you," West said from behind me.

I really didn't want to look up at either of them, but I couldn't help myself. I glanced back at West; I had to be sure. The voice was the same, but I wanted to see his face. Deep down, I was still holding on to a small slim hope that the boy who'd kissed me was better than this one standing behind me.

Unfortunately, in the light he was even more perfect than in the dark. I jerked my head back down to my map before he caught me looking at him. I hated him. I hated anyone who treated others as if their feelings didn't matter.

"You born that way?" Nash asked me, and I wished he'd give up. I didn't know what to do with him. He was very nice, but I wasn't going to talk to him.

West moved and suddenly he was standing in front of me, looking completely bored. The fact that his girlfriend had just broken up with him and ran off didn't seem to rank on his importance scale. It took a cold person to react that way.

I glanced at him and found his dark blue gaze on me. Long eyelashes framed his eyes. They weren't as startling as Nash's eyes—I was sure no one could have eyes as pretty as Nash's—but there was more there I had missed Friday night. Pain, fear, detachment. Again, the same thing I saw in my own eyes every time I looked in the mirror.

"Fuck, she's prettier up close," West said as he tilted his head to the side and studied me. "Makes me not care that she can't talk."

He was looking at me as if he hadn't held my face in his large hands Friday night. My stomach churned in a sick knot. I knew demented and cruel. I'd lived it. I'd witnessed it. And I feared it. If it weren't for the pain and fear in his eyes, I'd have slapped him. But I just wanted away from him. He wasn't a good person. Something had warped him. While I had chosen not to speak to deal with my pain, he had chosen to deal with his by hurting others.

"She's mute, dickhead. Not deaf," Nash snarled.

A crooked grin that didn't meet his eyes touched West's lips. Did his friends not see this? Did they not know he was hiding pain that haunted him and made him this horrible person?

"Don't mind me, sugar. I'm an asshole," he said, as if he were apologizing. But apologizing for what? Kissing me? Cheating on his girlfriend? Being an all-around heartless jerk with every word that came out of his mouth?

Those who were damaged weren't fixable. I knew that

all too well. Anyone who tried to fix him would fail. But people weren't born cruel. Life made them that way. At least that was what one of my counselors told me when she tried to talk to me about my father.

I made a blatant shift away from West and held my head high. The hard glare I shot him was more than any words could say. Thankfully, he got the message, and he turned and walked away.

I watched him go, wondering if there was someone who knew why he was acting out this way. Someone who knew the truth behind his cruel spirit. His girlfriend didn't, or she wouldn't have broken up with him like that. He held himself with a confidence that turned heads, and I guess no one noticed anything deeper.

Much as I knew he was bad news and wanted to hate him, I'd heard him talking to his mother. Heard him tell her he loved her. Heard the pain in his voice.

"Don't go there," Nash warned from beside me. "West ain't good, sweetheart. He's one of my best friends, but he's poison for girls like you. He don't care about anyone as much as he cares about West."

Nash didn't have to worry. I wasn't going anywhere near West. We had been close enough once, and he didn't even seem to remember. Our kiss wasn't something he thought about all weekend like I had.

Still, West needed to be saved. Someone had to get close to him, to reach him. No one had been able to save my father, and horror had followed in his path of destruction. West was in desperate need of help. That much I knew. I also knew I wasn't that person for him. I had my own demons to survive.

I Love You, Momma
CHAPTER 4

WEST

"Where's Brady?" Nash asked as he sat down at our table in the cafeteria.

"Ain't seen him. Probably with that good-looking cousin of his," I replied, trying to act as if I hadn't had her in my arms while her kiss shocked the hell out of me. Damn, that kiss had been sweet. I'd laid in bed that night thinking about how she'd felt. Her hands on my chest and her body leaning into me. For that one moment, I'd been able to forget. I hadn't thought about my life and what I was facing anytime I went home.

But then she'd made a small whimper, and it had snapped me out of my delirium. The girl couldn't speak, and I was pressing her against a tree and taking what I needed. God, I was a monster. She didn't deserve that.

I'd needed to get away from her, so I let her go and I'd walked off. I hadn't even been able to look at her when I broke away. One glimpse at those lips swollen from our kiss, and I'd have been right back at it. She wasn't just beautiful, she felt good too.

Not to mention that if Brady found out I'd kissed his cousin, we'd end up beating the shit out of each other. I deserved it, sure. She was too sweet for me.

"She really can't talk. I was in second period with her," said Asa Griffith, the other running back on the team. He'd been playing ball with us since elementary school. "I figure, if a girl looks like that and can't bitch, then she just might be perfect."

Nash, who was sitting down at the table, jumped in. "Don't be an ass. She's Brady's cousin." He sounded pissed. I'd seen the way he was looking at her this morning in the hall. He'd been taken with her real damn fast. And if I was honest with myself, I didn't like that.

"I'm being serious. She's gorgeous and can't talk. Does it get better than that?" Asa asked.

I wasn't going to say anything. As frustrating as Raleigh could be, I didn't wish a life of being mute on anyone. I knew Asa was joking, but it was too cold. He wasn't thinking about what he was saying.

"She was at the field party Friday night. Brady made it clear she was off mentally and not someone he wanted any of us moving in on," Ryker added to the conversation as he sat down across from his cousin. "She's not just mute, but, like, her mind isn't right."

Nash studied Ryker a minute as if he didn't agree with him. "She didn't seem off."

I agreed with him. Maggie wasn't off in the head, that much I knew. Brady was making that shit up. The girl was intelligent—her eyes were enough to prove that. There had been anger and disappointment in them as she glared at me. She had seen me at my worst, and I had wanted her to. After that kiss I wanted her to steer clear of me. I wasn't the kind of guy who got close to someone who was sweet.

Yes, seeing her at the party had sent a jolt of relief through me. But I'd let it register for only a moment before putting an end to it. Right now I couldn't deal with anything but my family. Last night, as I'd listened to my mother crying softly in the living room, I knew I didn't have it in me to be nice to any girl. Not even a girl like her.

Ryker rolled his eyes. "You know this because what? You looked at her? Sure, she's nice to look at, but if she's not right in the head, then it's screwed up to move in on her."

"Whatever, can we talk about something more interesting?" Gunner grumbled from the end of the table.

I didn't add to the conversation because I knew better, but also because I knew *her*. It had been like she'd seen through me. Seen my thoughts. And she understood. But she also expected more from me. That had been hard to swallow. For some crazed reason I didn't want to let her down. At the same time I wanted her to hate me enough so she never came near me again.

"We got a football game to win. We go and screw with our star quarterback's cousin, and we're messing with the team. All Brady needs in his head right now is football. Not stressing over your horny asses," Ryker said. It was a good point. If we were taking State this year, we needed Brady focused on one thing and one thing only: football.

I had to win the state championship for my dad. He wanted it. He'd been saying that my senior year was our year. I was determined to give him that. No matter what I had to do.

Forgetting that kiss wasn't going to be easy, but I didn't regret showing Maggie the ugliness from this morning. I'd lashed out and acted a way my mother would have been horrified by. But I'd seen the look in her eyes, and I knew she'd gotten the message. I wasn't a good guy. I wasn't anyone she needed to get to know or trust.

When I walked into the house after football practice that evening, the table was set like we were a normal, happy family. After I was born, this was the house my parents brought me home to from the hospital. It was the only home I had ever known. Yet the safety I once felt here was gone. Now I faced fear daily, hoping for a miracle.

My mother had prepared dinner just like she had most of my life. She was still pretending the best she could. I knew she prayed for that miracle too. Whenever she could, she acted as if life hadn't turned on us two years ago when my father was diagnosed. Tonight Momma even had fresh flowers on the center of the table. The basket beside them was full of freshly baked bread. She was baking a lot of bread lately. It was her way of coping, I had decided.

"You're home," she said with a smile that didn't meet her eyes. "How was practice?"

This was how she dealt with things: smiling, putting up a happy front. I wasn't sure if she was trying to help *me* get through this or if it was the only way she could handle it. Dad just let her do whatever; he didn't force her to face the truth. He adored her. Always had.

Our house wasn't big and fancy like the one she had grown up in. Yet she loved it. The way she took care of it and made it feel warm and inviting was proof she was proud of the life that Dad had given her. Not once did she speak about her past or the life she left behind when she married Dad.

"It was good. We're ready for Friday night. I feel confident we got this," was my reply. Because, like Dad, I couldn't let her down. If she wanted to pretend life was normal, then I would pretend with her.

"Dad eating with us?" I asked, wondering if he was better today. When I'd left this morning, he'd still been sleeping. No vomiting, and last night had seemed quiet.

She beamed at me, and the light in her eyes seemed almost real. "Yes, he is. He's just getting dressed now after his shower. He's looking forward to hearing all about practice. I think he's more excited about Friday's game than you are."

He was excited, but would he go? Last year he hadn't been this bad. He'd been able to sit up in the stands and watch. But now I couldn't imagine him sitting out there. Things had taken a bad turn the past month, and he wasn't getting better. I didn't want to shorten the time I had with him because he was going to my games when he should be resting.

"What's for dinner?" I asked, changing the topic. Dad and football were hard to talk about. I had grown up loving football because it was what Dad loved most in the world, second only to his family. It was how we bonded. All those days of him tossing me the ball in the backyard and the mornings we woke up early to go running together before school. It was us. An us that was slowly fading away.

"Meat loaf, mashed potatoes, and collard greens. Oh,

and of course corn bread. Your daddy loves his corn bread with his collard greens."

She was making all of Dad's favorites. He would hardly be able to eat anything. Didn't matter to her, though. She was doing it for him because she didn't know what else to do. I understood that.

I would sit at this table and talk to him about practice and the upcoming game like he would be there when we won the state championship. I wanted him there. I wanted to win it. I wanted him to see it happen. But I wasn't sure that was realistic.

All we could do was keep doing the things that made Dad happy. Even if inside we were both falling apart. He wasn't just a husband to Momma; he was her best friend. They had been inseparable my whole life. Next year I wanted to play SEC football, but could I leave her alone? With Dad not here, how did I continue with my dreams? With *our* dreams?

"Go on ahead and wash up. I'll get the glasses filled with ice, then I'll go see if your dad is ready to eat," she said, still smiling. Still trying to seem happy when I knew her heart was breaking just like mine.

"Yeah, okay," I replied. I didn't have it in me to say much else. I headed for the stairs then stopped. I needed her to know that she wasn't alone. That when this was over, she would have me. Momma had always seemed like this beautiful, fragile flower that Dad protected. But over the past year I had found out that she was made of steel. She never once cracked in front of Dad no matter how hard it got. She was right there beside him while I wanted to curl up and weep like a baby.

I turned around to face her. "I love you, Momma," I said, needing her to know. I was in this with her. She wasn't alone. When Dad was gone, I wouldn't let her be alone.

Her eyes filled with tears I knew she wouldn't shed. Then she nodded. "I love you too, baby."

That was enough for now. I wasn't ready to cry. Not in front of her. And I didn't think I could handle seeing her tears either.

CHAPTER 5

MAGGIE

I sat on my bed looking out the window. Tonight Brady had invited several guys over to watch game tapes—whatever that meant. Aunt Coralee had made sure I knew I was welcome to go down and watch with them if I wanted to. But I wasn't doing that to Brady.

Instead I was sitting here and watching to see if West would come over. As angry as he'd made me this morning, that look in his eyes he tried so hard to disguise had been nagging at me. I wanted to despise him, or even just be indifferent to him, but I couldn't seem to get him out of my thoughts.

I'd been so sure he was a monster after his performance

in the hallway. But later I'd watched him shove a guy against the wall and take a pair of glasses from him and then hand them back to a terrified-looking ninth grader. It had been so quick that if I hadn't been studying him, I would have missed it. Cruel, heartless people didn't do that. They didn't stand up for the weak. West was one big contradiction.

But I still wouldn't trust him. That much I knew. Just because he spoke kindly to his mother and helped a kid being picked on did not mean I would form any attachment to him. Yes, he had kissed me and, yes, I had liked it. And yes, I was curious about whatever secret he was keeping from everyone. But I wasn't one to let a guy turn my head. I had done that once in junior high school. He'd been a year older than I was and beautiful. I thought he really liked me, but then I'd found out he was just using me to get to my friend. After finding out he'd asked her to the homecoming dance, I had come home in tears. Mom had sat on the sofa with me and we'd eaten popcorn, chocolate ice cream with hot fudge, and pizza. She was always there when I hurt. She always knew how to make me smile. . . .

I shoved the memory away. I couldn't think about that. I missed her too much.

I pulled the blanket up over my arms and tucked it under my chin, then rested my head against the wall.

West's eyes were going to haunt me. Were all his friends blind to his behavior? Did they just accept it?

When I'd seen him kissing Raleigh this afternoon—she clearly didn't stay mad at him long and was rubbing all over him by the last bell—I'd wanted to be her for a second. Now that I knew how it felt to be in his arms, I had one weak moment where I'd wished he'd been the boy I thought he was Friday night. But then I remembered he was standing there kissing a girl he'd treated terribly. Was that his apology to Raleigh? Did she forgive him so easily? Probably. I'd seen that kind of warped relationship with my parents. If she only knew how unhealthy it could become.

Guys who looked like West made girls forget themselves. I had watched it so many times. When you are silent, you can observe so much more. I see others' mistakes more easily. And people feel safe saying things around me they wouldn't normally say because they know I won't repeat them or because they confuse being mute with being deaf.

For instance, two of my six teachers today had spoken extra loudly as if I couldn't hear them when they addressed me in class. It was comical. I was used to it by now, but it still made me laugh inside.

I wondered how it would feel to laugh again, to laugh right out loud. To feel the sound of it on my tongue. But knowing that my mother was gone and that I had made sure my father paid for his crime, could I ever laugh again? Could I hear my own voice and not break into a million pieces?

A knock at my bedroom door startled me, and I turned to see the knob slowly turn. I watched as the door eased open and Nash's face came into view. His eyes were just as startling against his dark skin as they had been earlier.

"You want company?" he asked, a sheepish grin tugging on his lips.

He was flirting with me. Several times today he'd appeared at my side and talked to me, knowing I wouldn't talk back. I hadn't expected that kind of attention, but I was certainly getting it from Nash. At first I was wary of him, but he'd been nothing but kind to me. He never went beyond my comfort zone, and I had watched him with other people. The others at school all seemed to love him. Even the teachers.

Although I wasn't in the mood for company, nor was I sure it was a good idea that he was up in my room, I shrugged. It wasn't an invite, exactly, but I hoped it wasn't rude, either.

"Good. They're boring me down there," he said.

I tried to manage a smile, but it didn't happen.

"You know," he continued as he sat down on the edge of my bed, facing me as I stayed curled up in the window seat, "school didn't suck today with you to look at."

I ducked my head and studied the blanket I was covered up with. He was going to flirt some more. I wasn't used to this. Sure, I'd had boyfriends before . . . before everything happened. That had been different, though. We hadn't been kissing or hanging out. It was more of a social thing that happened only at school or on the phone at night. My mother had been very overprotective, and I wasn't allowed to date until I was sixteen.

Once, I'd also been a cheerleader and had a lot of friends. But that all changed, and over the past two years I'd lost that part of me.

"I didn't mean to make you feel uncomfortable or embarrass you. I'm sorry. I was just trying to make your transition to a new school easier."

He was handsome and sweet. The kind of guy I would have liked in my former life. The kind of guy that any girl would like. I could ignore him and he would go away, but I wasn't going to be rude. He was my cousin's friend and, so far, my only almost-friend in town.

I reached for the notebook and pen I had left lying beside me after finishing my homework. He deserved something from me. I would like a friend here. Someone who didn't look at me as if I were a freak.

Thank you. For being nice to me. This day could've been harder than it was, but you were a friend.

I handed the notebook to him so he could read it.

He read my note, and a smile tugged up both corners of his mouth before he raised his gaze to meet mine. "You got a phone? So we can text?" he asked.

I nodded and reached into my pocket to pull it out. I had been given a phone by my godmother, Jorie, when I moved in with her after everything had happened. Two years with Jorie had been anything but comforting. I was in her way, and she had no idea how to deal with me. When I continued not to speak, she finally gave up and called my uncle Boone and asked him if he still wanted me. He and Aunt Coralee had responded immediately. It wasn't even one week before Jorie had me all packed up and ready to move. Since then, she hadn't even called to check on me. It's not like my number had changed; it was the same number she'd gotten me. The only difference was now my aunt and uncle were paying the bill.

Nash held out his hand. "Can I put my number in it?"

Again I nodded and let him take my phone from me.

He took a picture of himself then added his information. I heard a ding, and he grinned at me. "I texted myself. Now I have your number too. Can I take a picture of you to go with your contact info?"

I didn't really like the idea of him taking a photo of me, but I wasn't going to tell him no. I gave him a small nod, and then he held the phone up. "Smile," he said.

I didn't smile, but he took the photo anyway.

He chuckled. "That's okay. No need to smile."

The door opened, and we both turned to see Brady walk inside with a furious expression. "Get the hell out of here, Nash," he said, pointing at the door and glaring at his friend.

Nash held up both hands. "Calm down, bro. I was just talking to Maggie. We're friends aren't we, Maggie? Nothing more. I wasn't doing nothing else, I swear."

"Don't care. Get out," Brady repeated, still pointing at the door.

Nash stood up and glanced back at me, then held up his phone before winking and walking out the door.

Brady didn't say anything until Nash was gone. But once the door closed behind him, Brady turned to look at me. "Be careful, Maggie. These guys are my friends, but they don't always treat girls right. Hell, I don't always treat girls right. You . . . just keep your distance. Okay?"

He barely spoke to me, but now he seemed to think he had to protect me? I didn't need him telling me who I should be careful around. I understood others more than he did. If he didn't want me around his friends, that was fine. But demanding it of me wasn't fair. I lifted my chin and shot him a challenging glare. I had done everything to keep his parents from foisting me on him at every turn. But I wasn't going to take this behavior from him.

Brady's gaze found the notebook that Nash had left on the bed. Before I could reach it, he snatched it up. I waited while he read what I had said to Nash. It was meant to be nice and to thank Nash for today, but I knew Brady wouldn't see it that way.

He threw the notebook back down and let out a hard laugh that didn't sound amused at all.

He ran a hand through his messy hair. "I have a game to win Friday night. The whole damn town is counting on me to win it. But I can't focus on the game and make sure you're safe at the same time. I didn't ask to be anyone's guardian. I don't have time for this shit. So just please stay out of my world. Find friends who aren't on my team. And news flash: No guy is going to be your *friend*. Find some girls to be friends with. Jesus, how naive are you?" Then he walked out, closing the door hard behind him.

I wanted Brady to like me. I had tried to stay out of his way. I understood that my invading his life was unfair. But I wasn't okay with him speaking to me that way. Fine, I would keep my distance from his friends. Not because he ordered me to. Simply because, if they all were prone to acting like major jerks, I wanted nothing to do with them. I didn't need friends. I had survived without them long enough.

She Was All Over Me,
So I Let Her Enjoy Herself
CHAPTER 6

WEST

Raleigh wasn't waiting at my locker when I got to it today. I was relieved not to have to deal with her. Sometimes she was a nice distraction, but this morning I had been up since three with my dad. He'd gotten sick again, and I had woken up to the sound of my mother running down the hallway to get him a glass of water.

I had gone to help her, and we had all stayed up together. I was afraid to sleep. What if I went to sleep, and those were the last moments we had together? He was getting so thin and weak. The doctors couldn't do anything else. Last month they had sent him home with no hope. Just pain medication to ease him.

Facing school as if my life wasn't falling apart wasn't easy. And pretending like I wanted Raleigh around was something I definitely had no patience for right now.

I had just started pulling out my books when a dainty hand with cute pink fingernails touched the locker beside mine. It was Maggie. Someone who kept finding her way into my thoughts. Even though I was trying like hell to forget how she looked at me, like she saw something deeper than the asshole I'd shown her. Or how perfect she felt in my arms.

I glanced up to see her profile as she studied the lock and worked the combination. She really was something to look at.

With a small turn of her head, she peeked at me before angling back to her locker. I stood there, waiting for it to open, but after three tries she still hadn't gotten it.

"Move. Let me get it," I said. "You got the combination?"

She gave me her complete attention. Then she handed me her cell phone. I glanced down to see her combination on the screen. "Thanks. Now move back."

When she was out of my way, I quickly entered the combination and opened her locker. "There you go," I said just as her phone buzzed in my hand. Glancing down I saw Nash's face and the text Good morning, beautiful.

What the hell? Why was Nash texting her, and how the

hell had she gotten a picture of him on her phone? Brady had said she was off-limits.

I held the phone out to Maggie. "We got a lot riding on us this year to win State. We can't do it if our quarterback's cousin is messing around with the football team and screwing with our mojo. Back off." I sounded harsher than I'd meant to, but fuck that. I was exhausted.

She jerked the phone from my hand and glared at me. The whole point of acting like an asshole was so she'd hate me and stay away. But seeing that flash in her eyes made me regret the shit that had just come out of my mouth. Angry with myself, I turned and stalked off. Really it was Nash I was mad at. Nash, I should have corrected. Not Maggie. I had already made sure she kept her distance from me. She wouldn't even make eye contact with me now. I didn't have to keep being such an ass to her. Fact was, if I didn't act like a jerk around her all the time, I might forget and say something I shouldn't. Something true.

Nash was walking my way as I headed for first period. I knew he was going to find Maggie. That was bullshit. Brady had made it pretty damn clear he didn't want any of us going near his cousin. Because of his stupid-ass decision to ignore Brady's request, he'd made me snap and lash out at her.

"Don't," I snarled, and reached out to grab Nash's arm as he started to pass by me. "Brady doesn't want this and you need to respect that."

Nash tensed under my hand then jerked his arm free. "Didn't ask you, Ashby," he snapped, then kept going toward Maggie.

I couldn't worry about this. It wasn't something I was going to be able to control. If Nash wanted to do this, then I'd make sure he paid for it on the field today. We all would. And if he couldn't walk on Friday night, then I'd take up his slack. We could win this game without his stupid ass.

But we couldn't win it without Brady. And we were going to win it. I wasn't going to let my dad down.

"What's up with Raleigh being all over Jackson Hughs?" Gunner asked as he took the seat across from me in World History.

Last night Raleigh had apparently hooked up with Jackson Hughs, the only real soccer player we had at Lawton High School. He moved here from somewhere up north where they care about that shit. So now he was making a name for Lawton in soccer.

"Don't care," I replied honestly. When I first saw them together this morning on my way to first period, I stopped and waited for the hurt to come. Hell, for anything to come. After all, I'd been with Raleigh on and off for a year. But I never felt anything. Not one damn thing.

"Really? Y'all were all over each other yesterday in the hall," Gunner reminded me.

"She was all over me, so I let her enjoy herself." That was the truth—almost. Really I just needed the distraction she provided. I'd also been trying to get the memory of Maggie's kiss off me. It was haunting me and, damn, it was hard to forget.

Gunner chuckled. "Raleigh keeps looking over here. She's waiting on a reaction out of you."

She wasn't getting one. I shrugged and opened my textbook.

"That's cold, Ashby. Like, seriously cold-blooded. That's why you're a monster on the field. You just don't give a shit."

If he only knew. I gave a shit about something. Something that was tearing me apart.

"Nothing to care about," I replied.

"Nash said you were pissed at him about talking to Brady's cousin. I told him you were right."

This time I turned my head to actually look at Gunner. "I'll shut that down this afternoon on the field."

Gunner smirked. "You gonna let him walk away on both his legs?"

"No."

Gunner laughed in response. "I'll be Instagraming that shit."

Mr. Halter came into the room and started giving us reading instructions. Thank God, I'd get a nap in this class.

"My mom told me that girl saw her daddy kill her momma," Gunner whispered, leaning toward me. "That's fucked up."

What the hell was he talking about?

"Huh?" I asked as I turned back to him.

"Brady's cousin. She don't talk because she watched her daddy shoot her momma. He's in prison or on death row or something. My mom said she's mental now."

My stomach turned and twisted up in knots. I didn't want to believe that. Not for Maggie. Hell, not for anyone, but especially not for Maggie. She was kind. She didn't lash out or mistreat anyone. Even me, who she should have slapped at least three times now. There was no anger behind her gaze. Only a loneliness I wanted to ignore. But what Gunner was saying . . . That kind of horror would completely ruin a person.

Gunner's mother was famous for gossip and thought she knew everything in town. I wanted this to be wrong. But what if it was true? How was she living with that kind of nightmare?

Okay
CHAPTER 7

MAGGIE

You're still not answering my texts. What's up with that?

It was the fifth text from Nash today. I had been ignoring him, even if it was rude. I was done with everyone connected to Brady and the all-important football team. I had also seen West confront Nash in the hallway after jumping all over me about the text. I didn't have time for this drama. I wanted no part of it.

I knew I should explain to Nash why I wasn't going to be texting him. He deserved an explanation. I'd do that during lunch. Yesterday Brady had sat with me outside at the picnic tables, but it had been awkward. He obviously didn't want to.

I'd sent him a text this morning telling him he didn't need to sit with me at lunch today. I was ready to figure this out on my own. He had responded with a simple yeah.

"You gonna answer him?" I recognized West's voice.

I glanced up to see him walking beside me. His eyes weren't on me, just glaring straight ahead. From the frown on his face I knew he was unhappy with Nash texting me. Not like I cared about that—I was ignoring Nash to detach myself from all things Brady. Since that was what would give me the most peace at home and at school. But I was tired of people telling me what to do. Especially this person. Someone who had no right to tell me who I could and couldn't talk to.

I slipped my phone back into my pocket.

"Good girl. Ignore him. Save us all a helluva lot of trouble. I'll make him pay for this shit if he keeps it up," West warned without once looking at me.

My face felt hot as his condescending words rang in my head. He had no right to speak to me that way. Just because I didn't speak, didn't make me ignorant.

"Okay!" I snapped. It took only a second for the realization to wash over me that I'd spoken out loud. He'd made me so angry, I just blurted it out. My skin broke out into a cold sweat. I would not lose it. I was fine. It was just one word.

His eyes were on me now. Confusion and disbelief as he stared down at me. I glanced up at him, wanting desperately to run from this or somehow erase it. The word had just burst free without difficulty or pain. But my memories . . . I didn't want those to come out with the sound of my voice.

"Did you just . . ." He trailed off as if trying to decide whether he had really heard me speak. I didn't confirm or deny it. I simply stood there staring up at him. I wouldn't say more. Maybe he would think he imagined it.

He shook his head and then turned and stalked off down the hallway. The crowd parted for him, too. Just like it did for Brady. I reached up and touched my lips with my fingertips. What was it about West Ashby that made my mouth have a mind of its own? First I let him kiss me without even knowing him. And now I said something without even thinking about it.

When he turned the corner and was finally gone from my sight, I inhaled and dropped my hand back to my side. I had actually said something. That had been a piece of me I'd lost— the girl who didn't take whatever anyone threw at her but who stood up for herself—and she'd broken free for a moment. I hadn't had that instinct, or any control over my voice, in two years. And West, even if it was because he acted like a jerk, had made that possible.

My phone vibrated in my pocket again. All I could hope

for was that West didn't tell anyone what he'd heard. I wasn't ready to speak. I didn't think I'd ever be able to hear my voice again. I wasn't ready for any connection with people.

I pulled my phone back out and sent a text to Nash: Please leave me alone. I don't want to be friends. Think about how this would affect Brady. Stop texting me. And talking to me.

I pressed send and went to find the library. I would just start reading during lunchtime. Making myself as invisible as possible.

The pep rally was after lunch on Friday. Cheerleaders had spent the day in their uniforms and doing cheers in the hallways to drum up school spirit. The football players' lockers were easy to recognize, since they had been decorated with balloons, hearts, and posters.

Today Brady walked through the halls as if he owned the place. More so than he usually did. His name was chanted often, and he beamed whenever a chant started up. Between classes the cheerleaders even had the entire hallway doing cheers for him. I couldn't imagine that after all this, we even needed a pep rally. I'd been a cheerleader once, but I didn't recall ever having this much spirit on game day. Seemed like overkill.

After Tuesday no one had really spoken to me the rest of the week. I managed to fade into the walls. Nash was no

longer texting me or seeking me out. When I passed him in
the halls, he didn't even glance my way. It was what Brady
wanted, and it was best for me. Still, being invisible only
added to my loneliness. Finding friends was hard when you
didn't speak. People didn't know what to do with you. I
could see the way they watched me and could hear them
whisper about me. Reaching out and making friends wasn't
something I was brave enough to do.

Then there was West. I'd expected him to say something to me about that one spoken word, but he never did.
He also ignored me. If I didn't know that I was in fact
visible to the human eye, I would've assumed I truly had
disappeared. The only interaction I had with West was
when I dropped a book while walking down the crowded
hallway. Out of nowhere he bent down, stopping traffic
to pick it up for me. He hadn't made eye contact with me,
though. He'd just walked away.

Facing an entire gym full of loud, excited students as
they hooted for the cheerleaders and football team wasn't
appealing, but I had to go. My aunt wouldn't be picking me
up until it was over. She'd want to know if I enjoyed the
pep rally, and I would have to lie.

I tucked my book bag under my legs after getting a seat
on the far end of the bleachers near the door. When it was
time to leave, I would have an easy exit out of the gym.

Scanning the team's faces, I found Brady immediately. He seemed more focused and less exuberant than the other guys, who were interacting with the crowd. People were chanting different names, and the guys were enjoying it. I continued looking through the team, not admitting to myself that I was looking for West. His dark head was nowhere to be found. I had just started scanning the whole team again when I heard giggles around me.

"God, I want to be her," said a girl sitting in front of me. I wasn't sure who "her" was. But as the girl's friend turned her head to look toward the doors, I followed her gaze and saw West in the doorway with Raleigh wrapped around him.

"He always takes her back. It's so frustrating. She's not that hot," the first girl added.

"I disagree," a guy broke in. "She's smoking,"

West tore his mouth off Raleigh's and grinned. Then he put her down and entered the gym like he was the king and we were all his royal subjects.

"I want him." The first girl sighed, and her friend laughed as they made more remarks about West's body and the other things they loved about him.

When he got to the center of the gym, he turned and smiled at the screaming crowd. Sure, his smile was beautiful, but it wasn't real. It was lifeless and fake. Did no one see that? Was I the only one?

An argument started up beside me, and I noticed a guy with short blond hair and glasses trying to get the girl on my left to move over. She was rolling her eyes at him, but she eventually scooted away from me. The blond guy slid in beside me then tucked his book bag to his left, causing the girl to complain some more.

Finally he turned his gaze to me and smiled sheepishly. "Hey, I'm Charlie. We have second and fourth period together. Lunch, too, but you always seem to disappear during lunch," he said. "I also know you don't talk. I just wanted to introduce myself. And if you need anything or want to see a movie sometime, I'm available."

"Seriously? That's your pickup line?" asked the girl he had moved over. She rolled her eyes again before looking away from us and back at the football team.

"I'm not good at this kind of thing. I actually suck at it. But I . . . I was just wondering if maybe you'd like . . ." He trailed off as his cheeks turned pink. He was really cute. And nice. His eyes weren't haunted, and I would bet he had a happy home life. With two parents who loved him. And no demons to carry around like I did.

He also wasn't a football player. Something I liked a lot.

I reached for my note pad, which was tucked in the pocket of my book bag.

It's nice to meet you, Charlie. I'm Maggie.

His grin grew. "Yeah, I know your name. I asked already. Not stalkerish or anything. Just curious. You're new and all. We've all gone to school together most of our lives, so when someone new comes along . . ."

He trailed off as his cheeks went pink again. I didn't have a response for that.

He chuckled and dropped his gaze to his hands. "So, what about that movie? You up for a movie?"

A movie . . . as in a date. I'd never been on a date. Did I want to? Was I ready for this?

I had said one word this week. West had brought it out of me without meaning to. I hadn't fallen apart or ended up in a corner because of it. I was stronger now. But was I ready to date?

What if it was just West? What if I spoke to someone else, and hearing my voice sent me into a darkness I couldn't find my way out of?

I looked back at the notebook in my lap then wrote.

Maybe.

That was all I could promise right now.

Let's Own This Season

CHAPTER 8

WEST

It was the first time in my life I'd played a game without my dad there. Our win was the only thing the others were thinking about when it was over, so luckily, no one noticed except Brady. I'd shrugged it off and told him Dad wasn't feeling well.

I ran in two touchdowns, but my dad wasn't there to see them. He hadn't been in his spot cheering me on. He hadn't been at the fence with his big grin when I came running to the sidelines. He hadn't been there because he'd had a fever and was on so much pain medicine, he wasn't even lucid.

He hated taking the pain meds—he liked being there mentally with us—but he'd been in so much pain last night, Mom had forced him to take them. Then, when he finally went to sleep, she'd fallen into my arms and sobbed. I had never seen her like that before, had never seen her break down.

Facing today's game had been the last thing I wanted to do. Knowing I would get to go home and tell my dad about it had been the only way I'd been able to play. I wanted to tell him something that would make him smile. I wanted him to believe in me. He and I had shared my dreams for so long. I didn't want him to know I was losing those dreams. Because without him, I wouldn't care anymore.

Not to mention Mom would need me when he was gone.

I hadn't looked for Raleigh after the game. I'd gone straight to my truck, determined to get the hell away from all of them. All their joy over our win. I couldn't be happy. My dad hadn't been there. Winning didn't mean as much anymore.

Facing my dad while my emotions were so raw wasn't a good idea. But going to the field party where the team would be celebrating seemed fucking pointless. I couldn't celebrate. I just wanted to forget. I wanted my old life back. I wanted my dad healthy.

After driving around for almost an hour, lost in the pain that had become part of me, my truck drove down the familiar dirt road to the field party. It was here or home, and I couldn't go home just yet. I needed a few beers, and I needed to forget.

Everyone was already here. The loud shouts and laughter had once been welcome sounds. Now I hated them. None of my friends had worries except winning a football game. They didn't know what fear was. None of them. These were the best fucking years of their lives. Once, they'd been mine, too.

I closed my truck door and stared at the bonfire through the trees. I would have to walk in there and put on a smile I didn't feel. I would have to talk about a game I played with everything I had but only because I wanted to be able to tell my dad about it. Not because my heart was in it.

I didn't fit in anymore. With any of them.

But where else would I go?

Drinking would ease the pain some. Nothing would take it all away.

I would pretend. It was what I did best lately.

Heading into the open field, I found a beer and made my way over to my friends. Raleigh was here already. I could see her over with the soccer boys. I knew she was mad, and that was her way of getting back at me. I just didn't care.

"Where you been, man? We've been replaying the awe-someness that was Ashby tonight, and you weren't even here to glory in it!" Ryker yelled out to me as I walked toward them.

"Had some things to do first," I replied with a grin that hinted I'd been doing some*one* rather than some*things*. I'd let them think what they wanted. Anything but the truth.

Laughter followed my comment.

"Guess that's why Raleigh moved over to soccer boy land," Nash replied. He'd been pissed at me for a day or two, but after practice on Thursday we'd both agreed I was right. He had to focus on football not Brady's cousin.

I shrugged and took a seat down on the tractor tire that Ryker was sitting on. "Whatever," I replied.

Next to me, Ryker started talking. "But seriously, Nash. You got to quit looking for her. She's okay. She's here, and she's not your business. Brady will be back in a minute with Ivy's drink, and if he thinks you're looking for his cousin, he'll get pissy."

I turned my attention to Nash. I thought he had backed off that.

Nash held up both his hands. "Easy, I was just seeing who was here. Not looking for anyone."

"Bullshit," Ryker muttered.

"She's here?" I asked, wondering why she came to these parties if she was just going to hide in the corner.

"Brady said his momma made him bring her. She doesn't want to come. He feels bad for her," Ivy said with a shrug, as if she couldn't care less.

"Pisses me off that he doesn't let her sit with us." Nash sounded aggravated.

"Not. Your. Business," was Ryker's response. I wanted to agree with Ryker, but Nash was right too. Brady was wrong just bringing her here and leaving her all alone. It was cruel.

"Uh-oh, here comes drama," Ivy said with a smile, then looked at me.

"Well, shi-it," Ryker drawled as I turned to see Raleigh walking our way.

Her hair was messy from fooling around with the soccer guy. What was she heading over here for? I liked her better over there.

"Y'all confuse the hell out of me," Nash said. "Today at the pep rally I thought she was going to suck your face off. Now she's sucking someone else's face off."

I grabbed my beer and stood up. I was leaving. I didn't want her shit tonight. I had bigger issues than Raleigh.

"I'm out," I said.

"You leaving?"

"Already?"

"You did that last week!"

They all seemed surprised. I just nodded and held up my beer. "Good game. Let's own this season," I said, then headed to the woods and my truck.

I Have Nightmares Every Night
CHAPTER 9

MAGGIE

I sat on the back of Brady's truck, watching my feet swing back and forth. The noise from the party wasn't as loud back here. Tonight Brady hadn't driven his truck up to the party; he'd left it parked with the other vehicles in the wooded area just off the dirt road. I knew it was because he wanted me to have somewhere to stay. He was trying to make this easier on me. He'd even brought me a bowl of pretzels and a soda a little while ago. He'd seemed concerned. But all of a sudden some girl with long dark hair drove up, and he got angry. He stalked off after that.

The girl just stood there for a while, staring after Brady

before getting back into her car and driving away. Strange. I had never seen her before.

"You might have the best seat in the place." West Ashby's voice startled me. "Don't mind me. I'm just tired of acting like I give a shit out there. I needed to be alone. Since you don't talk, that makes it better. Someone I can talk to who keeps quiet. Might be fucking perfect." He took a long drink of his beer then sat down beside me on the truck bed.

Was he drunk? He had to be. Surely, he was aware that I was the last person who wanted to be his company. I wasn't his friend. I would never be his friend.

"Maybe I should stop talking. Then I wouldn't have to pretend to give a fucking shit. Bet that's easy, huh? Not having to react to anything. I envy you."

Envy me? Seriously? He was going to sit here and make jabs at me when he didn't even know me. He had no clue why I chose not to speak. To say he envied me made me want to stand up and scream in his face. No one on earth should ever envy me. Ever.

"But I did hear some stuff that, if it's true, maybe your shit's worse than mine." He shook his head and sighed. "Naw, probably ain't. Gunner's momma is a gossip. Half the stuff comes out of her mouth is false. God knows she's talked about my momma enough."

He looked as if he were talking to himself now. His eyes were focused on something out in the darkness. Pain was etched across his face. He wasn't trying to hide anything out here, not like he did all the other times I'd been around him. This was the first time I really saw him, the guy he didn't reveal to anyone. His mask was gone, and there was heaviness in his voice and darkness in his eyes.

"Didn't come to my game tonight. He couldn't. Hell, he can't even go to the damn bathroom without help now. Much less watch me play. First time in my life he hasn't watched me play. Every touchdown I scored I did it for him. So I'd have something good to tell him tonight. But here I sit like a fucking pussy because going home to see him scares the hell out of me."

Him who? I wanted to ask but was afraid to. His emotions were too raw. This wasn't the jerk he showed the world. This was the guy underneath that. He was allowing me to see him. His pain. His fears. But why?

"When I was born, Momma said he brought a football to the hospital for me. Ran right out and bought it when they said it was a boy. He put it in my crib with me from that day on. I loved football, but it was because I loved him. He's always been my hero. Now he's gonna fucking leave me. And Momma." He let out a hard laugh clearly full of agony. "How's she gonna make it? He's her world. Always has been. I can't imagine my momma without my dad. She'll be so lost. I won't be enough. I just—" He dropped his head in his hands and let out a groan. "Fuck, I'm scared, Maggie. You know what it's like, to be scared?" he asked, lifting his head to look at me for the first time.

I knew. I knew all too well. I knew terror and fear. I knew demons that haunted you at night instead of the sweet dreams we believed in as children. I knew more than he could imagine.

I nodded. "Yes," I whispered hoarsely, desperate to assure him he wasn't alone. My voice sounded strange yet familiar.

This was the second time I had spoken to him. Once because he infuriated me, and now because I understood he needed to know he wasn't alone. Pain came to all of us at some time or another. It was how we learned to cope with it that determined our future. In this moment I chose to speak. Silence was normally how I coped, but for the first time since I'd witnessed my father kill my mother, I wanted to speak. I wanted to reassure someone else.

His eyes widened. "You talked," he said, staring at me intently. "Again."

I didn't say anything in response. I had spoken because he needed me to. But to talk, just for conversation? I couldn't do that. I was still afraid to hear my voice.

"Is it true? About what Gunner told me . . . Did you see your dad . . ." He trailed off. He knew my past. Someone had found out and was spreading it around. I knew it would happen eventually.

I thought about my answer. I didn't talk about that night with anyone. Remembering was too hard. Too painful for any human to endure. But West was losing a parent too.

So I nodded. I wouldn't give him any more than that. I couldn't put into words what I'd seen. Not again.

"Shit. That's tough," was all he said.

We sat there in silence for several minutes, staring off into the darkness.

"My dad's dying. Doctors can't do anything for him anymore. Sent him home to just . . . die. Every day I watch him fall away a little more. Further from our grasp. Further from us. He's in so much pain, and there isn't anything I can do. I'm afraid to go to school because, what if he dies while I'm gone and I never see him again? But then, like right fucking now, I'm afraid to go home because he may have gotten worse and then I'd have to see that. I have to see the man I adore wasting away. Leaving this life. Leaving us."

My mother's death had been fast. Immediate. She hadn't suffered except for that one moment I was screaming at my dad to stop while he pointed a gun at her. I know she suffered then. She suffered for me and what I would see.

But I didn't know what it felt like to watch a parent die slowly before your eyes. To go to sleep at night and not know if they'd be there the next morning. My heart ached for him. Losing someone you loved was hard. The hardest thing in life. West wasn't a nice person. He could be downright cruel. But the emotion in his voice was hard to ignore. I didn't want to feel anything for him, even sorrow, but I did.

"No one knows," he continued. "I can't tell them. All they know is, Dad had surgery and is on disability now. He doesn't work anymore. I blew it off when I told them, like it was no big thing." He laughed again, a hard, brutal sound that held no humor. "These women in this town never accepted my momma She ain't got any friends to talk to except your aunt, and I don't think she's even told Coralee. When Dad's gone . . . I'll be it. How do I do that? How can I be enough?"

Nothing I could do would ease this pain. Nothing anyone could do would make it better. So I reached over with my hand and covered his. It was the only thing I knew to do. Other than speak, and he didn't need that. I wasn't sure I could anyway.

He started to turn his hand over to hold mine when he stopped and pulled away. Then he stood up as if he were going to leave. I didn't want him to leave like this. He had opened up to me about the demons he was facing. He had laid his secrets bare. He would go home to that nightmare and live it again and again until it was over. He didn't want to tell anyone, yet he'd told me. Had he seen in my eyes what I'd seen in his? The sorrow and anger? The regret and suffering?

"I have nightmares every night," I said. "I see my mother die over and over."

CHAPTER 10

WEST

She hadn't whispered this time. The sweet Southern drawl in her voice was beautiful. It wasn't high-pitched, just a touch deeper.

The words she'd spoken were so incredibly revealing, it hurt to think about her reliving something like that every night. I didn't know what to say to her. My dad was dying of cancer. It was ripping me apart. But she'd seen her father murder her mother. That kind of brutality was beyond anything I could imagine.

She closed her eyes tightly and took a deep breath. I watched her closely, unable to take my gaze off her. I was afraid she'd move or vanish. And I needed her. Right now at least, I needed someone to know my pain. Someone to understand it.

"It never leaves you . . . the hurt," she said as she opened her eyes to look at me. "But you learn to live and you learn to deal with the loss. You do what you have to survive."

I understood now. Why she didn't talk . . . why she remained mute. It was about not reliving that moment. Not talking or laughing. Just keeping to herself. Until now. With me.

"You're talking to me. Why me?"

Her gaze flicked over my shoulder, and I could see the sorrow in her eyes. "Because you needed me to. You need to know someone else has lived through pain like yours."

I took a step toward her. "When you lost your mom, was someone there for you?" I asked, hoping she said yes. I didn't like the idea of her battling this kind of horror alone.

She looked back at me. "No. No one understood. No one saw what I did. No one lived through what I had. I would have talked to them. But there was no one to understand. Keeping quiet is how I survived."

I kept quiet too. Just not the way she did. I kept my father's illness a secret. I didn't have friends over, and I didn't tell them what was happening. My dad had still been fine last year when I'd had a party at my house the week after spring training. Then this summer things started going downhill. The last three weeks they had gone from bad to worse.

Eventually everyone would find out, I knew that. This wasn't a secret I could keep forever. But I didn't want to tell them. I didn't want to see the sympathy in their eyes. I didn't want them trying to console me when they didn't understand.

"Maggie!" Brady's voice came through the darkness. I saw Maggie tense up and give me a small smile before getting off the truck bed and heading toward her cousin's voice. She hadn't wanted him to catch me out here with her.

But I hadn't been ready to see her go.

All weekend I found myself thinking about Maggie. When Dad would get sick, I reminded myself that I was strong enough to handle this. I would be there for my mother. I wasn't a scared little boy anymore. If Maggie could survive what she had seen, I needed to man up and be what my dad needed.

Monday morning I left my mother tucked in beside my dad's frail body and headed to school with Maggie on my mind. Her voice had been in my head, reminding me that the pain was something I had to learn to deal with. I had to make it through the nightmare I was living. She was a walking testament to the fact I could do this.

Seeing her standing at the locker beside mine was a relief. I had needed to see her. We had talked all of ten minutes, and already I had grown attached to her. She understood. I hadn't realized how badly I needed that. Someone to understand.

"Morning," I said as I moved to stand next to her and open my locker.

She glanced at me and smiled. But nothing more. No words. No smooth, warm voice to calm me. Just a small smile. Fuck that. I wanted to hear her talk.

"You not gonna talk to me?" I asked, still watching her in case she whispered and I missed it.

She turned her attention back to her locker and got out a notebook then closed it before glancing back at me. For a moment I thought she was going to talk, but she simply shook her head and then walked away. Leaving me there.

I had focused on her words and her voice all weekend to overcome my demons and face them head on. And she acts like we never spoke. Like she doesn't know my secrets. Like I don't know hers.

Bullshit.

I grabbed my first-period books and slammed my locker, and then I went after her. Just before I reached her, a hand wrapped around my arm. Jerking it free, I turned to glare at Brady. He didn't look happy.

"Are you going after Maggie?"

I could lie, but that was pointless. "Yeah," I replied.

"Not you, too," he snarled. "Why the fuck can't y'all leave her alone? She's mute. She's seen shit none of us can comprehend, and she isn't a plaything for you. So go find someone else to chase after. My cousin is off. Limits."

I couldn't explain to him that I just wanted to talk to her again. He had no idea she'd talked to me. She wasn't talking to anyone else. She'd only talked to me.

But even if she didn't want to speak to me anymore, I didn't want to stay away from her. Maggie made me feel stronger. She reminded me that I wasn't alone in this world. That others had gone through this too. That I could be what my momma needed me to be . . . what my dad needed me to be.

"Fine. Whatever. I don't have time for this shit," I replied before stalking off the other way.

Out of nowhere, Raleigh stepped in front of me. "You didn't call all weekend," she said, sticking her bottom lip out and pouting.

I hadn't called her because I hadn't needed her to distract me. "You looked like you moved on Friday night," I replied, shoving past her and walking toward my class.

"I was trying to make you jealous. You left me again, West. You never think about me. You just leave me."

She was right that I didn't think about her. She deserved more. I wasn't able to be what Raleigh deserved. In the beginning I had been attracted to her. She was fun and exciting, and I didn't think about my dad's treatments when we were together. But that had only lasted a little while. Soon it just became about sex. I used her to forget for a moment. I felt guilty about it, but she'd seemed happy with things. She liked being my girlfriend.

What I knew now was that she deserved more than I was able to give her. It was time I cut her loose and let her go find a guy who could make her happy. All we did was fight.

"Then I'm not the guy for you. I'm never going to remember to check on you, Ray. I'm never going to be thinking about you. It's not me. I don't do that. So go find a guy who does. I sure as shit can't make you happy."

The look in her eyes wasn't heartbreak. We weren't in love. Although she liked to tell me she loved me often, I knew she didn't. Who could love an asshole?

"I love you," she said as if she'd read my thoughts.

I shook my head. "No, Ray, you don't. I'm not lovable. Let's stop this. You just get hurt with me, and that'll never change. So this time, it really is over. Go find a guy who can be what you need. You deserve that. I can't be that guy. Not for you. Not for anyone."

I didn't wait for her to reply before I turned and walked into first period.

I realized as I sat down that the words I'd just said to Raleigh were true. I couldn't be mad at Brady for protecting Maggie from me. But maybe he'd let us be friends. I just needed a fucking friend right now. Not a girlfriend. How could I explain that to him?

Times Like These, I Was Glad I
Wasn't Expected to Say Something
CHAPTER 11

MAGGIE

I walked into the cafeteria. I was choosing not to starve my way through lunch in the library. After a week at school I felt safer. Like I knew how things worked and what to expect. I didn't feel like all eyes were on me anymore.

Well, that wasn't exactly the whole story. Truth was, I wanted to see West. He hadn't been at his locker since this morning, and when I passed him in the hall, he looked right through me. Sure, I'd not spoken this morning, but I wasn't sure I could. Would I have a meltdown if I weren't trying to help him? Maybe speaking only worked when he needed me to speak. Maybe it was West's pain that triggered my ability to speak without losing my grip.

In the days after my mother's death I had sat in a corner and screamed when anyone came near me. I knew what I was doing was crazy, but I couldn't stop myself. A helpless fear had consumed me. I was in so much agony, I couldn't be spoken to or handle anyone getting close to me.

When I was finally able to coax myself out of the corner and stop reliving the nightmare over and over in my head, I managed to function. But I still wouldn't speak. It was the one thing that saved me. I could deal if I didn't hear the sound of my voice.

"So, about that date we discussed at the pep rally?"

I turned from my place in the food line to see Charlie grinning at me. "I looked for you after the game Friday night, but you were nowhere to be found."

Yeah, because my aunt and uncle shipped me off with Brady.

"Since you don't have a notebook at the moment, I'll do all the talking," he continued. "I was thinking maybe Saturday we could go to Nashville for the day. It's only an hour drive away. There's an excellent place I like to eat there, and then I have tickets to the Grand Ole Opry that night. Dierks Bentley is going to be there."

I had no idea who Dierks Bentley was, but I knew what the Grand Ole Opry was. I was pretty sure everyone in the South knew what that was. But an entire day with Charlie . . . in Nashville? I wasn't sure my aunt and uncle would be okay with that.

"Just think about it. I promise we'll have fun. And I talk enough for both of us."

I started to smile, when my gaze locked on a person looking directly at me. West.

He was sitting at the table were Brady sat, along with the other football players. They were all allowed to come in early and get their trays so they could leave earlier and head to the field house.

"You know West Ashby? Well, yeah, you probably do considering he's your cousin's best friend."

I tore my gaze away from West's and moved up as the line did. I had come to see him, and there he was. Looking right at me. I wasn't invisible to him now. Maybe he had forgiven me for not talking this morning.

"You sitting with anyone?' Charlie asked.

I shook my head.

"Want to keep me company?"

I thought about that. Charlie was a nice guy, and he was okay with the fact I wasn't going to talk to him. I nodded.

That got a smile from him. "Awesome," he replied.

We both took our trays after choosing what we wanted, and I let Charlie lead the way. I had no idea where to go sit. Luckily, he had a table where he always sat, and there were several other people there who greeted him as we approached. I was going to meet Charlie's friends, it seemed.

"Hey, guys, this is Maggie. Maggie, this is Shane." He pointed to a redhead with a lot of freckles and a pair of very large glasses. "May." May was a brunette with short curly hair and a forced smile. She wasn't happy I was here— I didn't need her to say anything to know that; it was all over her face. "Dick—yes, seriously that is his name. His mother hates him." The dark-haired guy grinned at me, and I could tell he was curious. The light in his green eyes said he found something amusing.

"Maggie and I met at the pep rally Friday, and I am currently trying to talk her into going to Nashville with me Saturday."

May's shoulders snapped back, and fire lit her eyes. "You're taking her to see Dierks Bentley?" she asked, sounding completely horrified.

"Oh boy," Dick said with a chuckle.

Charlie completely ignored her reaction. His smile stayed in place as he sat down then nodded for me to sit beside him. "Sure am. She's going to love it," was his response.

Shane snorted as he took a drink of his milk. It appeared Shane and Dick were both having a hard time keeping it together. But Charlie continued to be oblivious to it all.

"Uh-oh," Dick said as he dropped his sandwich to the tray. His eyes went wide.

"What?" Charlie asked as I turned to see what Dick was looking at.

Brady.

He was looking at Brady. Because Brady was coming this way. And he didn't look happy. His tray was tight in his grip, and the clench of his jaw was hard to miss.

"Maggie," Brady said as he sat down in the empty seat to the right of me.

I just stared at him. What was he doing?

"There's another one," Shane whispered, and I shifted my gaze from Brady to see West walking our way. He was watching me closely and also looked unhappy.

When his tray clanked loudly on the table, everyone but Brady jumped.

"What are you doing?" Brady asked him as West took the seat across from Brady.

"Same thing you're doing," he replied, then turned his gaze to me for a second before glaring at Charlie.

"I'm making sure my cousin is all right," Brady replied.

West shifted his gaze back to me. It softened. "Me too."

Brady muttered a curse word, and West just smirked as he picked up his burger and took a bite. I was used to Brady being a little overprotective, but West? I didn't understand why he was here. Because we had talked? Did his opening up to me and my actually speaking make him feel as if he had to look out for me? I didn't need either of them to keep me safe. Especially from someone like Charlie.

"Great. You got the jock squad over here now," May grumbled.

Brady and West both ignored her comment.

"Sooo, how about that game Friday night, eh?" Dick said with a nervous smile.

Brady lifted his head to shoot Dick an annoyed glance before going back to his meal.

"I don't think they're here to talk to us," Shane whispered loudly.

No one said anything for a few moments. Awkward silence was something I had grown used to. But right now I really wanted Charlie to be chatty.

"You ever been to the Grand Ole Opry?" Charlie asked me.

I started to shake my head when Brady spoke up. "No. She hasn't."

I glanced over at my cousin, who was eating his food like he was mad at it.

"Oh, well. You're gonna love it," Charlie said brightly. He didn't seem at all affected by Brady's rude behavior.

"I still can't believe you're taking her. You hardly know

her. You know I've been dying to see Dierks Bentley in concert forever," May said, sounding hurt.

Charlie glanced at me, and I saw the frustration in his eyes. He didn't want to let May down. Why had he asked me, then? I didn't have to go.

"She's not going with you. Anywhere," Brady said in his less-than-jolly tone.

It was times like these I was glad I wasn't expected to say anything.

CHAPTER 12

WEST

The guys were going to watch the video of Friday night's game at Brady's tonight. His mom would make tacos and chocolate cake. She always did. It was something we did every week during football season.

I hadn't planned on going. Hospice had come today for the first time. Dealing with that was harder than I'd thought it would be. Dad had needed the pain meds so much this past week, he wasn't coherent enough to even ask about Friday night's game. I'd sat in his room and told him anyway. Hoping that, in his drugged sleep, he'd heard me.

That he was proud of me.

Soon I wouldn't be able to sit in his room and talk to him at all.

Getting away from the heaviness in my house was necessary to keep sane. Having a stranger there, taking care of dad while my mother sat beside him, holding his hand, was too much.

So I ran. And I felt guilty about it.

Parking my truck outside Brady's house, I realized I was the last one here. They all probably thought I wasn't coming. When I walked inside, there would be laughter and joking. None of them had any worries or pain to deal with. It was all good food and football.

I glanced up at the window that had been Brady's before Maggie had moved in. I wondered if she was up there now or if she was downstairs eating tacos with the guys. If it were up to her, she wouldn't be. But if it was up to Coralee, I had a feeling she would be forced to sit down there with them.

I didn't know a lot about Maggie, but I watched her. So much so that I was afraid someone was going to notice and say something about it. Watching her eased my mind. Even from afar she was enough to help me breathe. I was becoming dependent on a girl I hardly knew.

Footsteps snapped me out of my thoughts. I turned to see who it was, and my gaze found her.

"Brady doesn't think you're coming. Aunt Coralee pulled Brady aside this afternoon and told her about your dad. She knows. Brady was upset and wanted to come see you, but she said to give you time. That you needed to tell him yourself." Maggie's sweet voice made my chest warm. That wasn't something I was familiar with anymore. The coldness had been there for so long now.

She had her long hair tucked behind her ears, and she was staring at the house like I had been. There was a peace that came with her presence. I didn't understand it because she carried so much heaviness. But for me, she brought peace.

"Hospice came today. Feels like the end," I told her.

She tilted her head back and looked up at me. At six-foot-two, I towered over her five-foot-five frame. "The end hurts," she said simply.

She wasn't sugarcoating it. She wasn't telling me I had to be strong. She was just being honest. She knew that words meant nothing right now. I reached over and covered her small hand with mine.

"It hurts like hell," I replied.

She let me hold her hand as we stood there silently. This was what I needed today. Having her beside me, knowing she understood.

"Thanks. For talking to me," I whispered, as if someone would hear me.

She turned her hand in mine and squeezed. "I'm here whenever you need to talk."

"You didn't talk to me today at school," I reminded her.

"You didn't need me to then."

"I did. You just didn't realize how much."

The front door of the house opened, and Maggie quickly moved her hand from mine.

Brady stood there staring. At first I expected him to yell at me for being out here with Maggie. But then I saw it wasn't anger in his eyes. It was sadness. He was sad for me. Then there was the sympathy I didn't want.

"He loves you. He's going to feel bad for you. Let him," Maggie whispered so quietly, I doubted Brady could tell she had said anything from where he stood.

Let him.

She said I should let him feel sorry for me. Because he loved me. I could do that. I had to. There was no way to keep it from happening. Knowing there was one person who understood my pain in a way no one ever could was enough.

"Stay with me," I asked her, not taking my eyes off Brady.

"Okay," was her soft reply.

Brady walked toward us. Maggie stayed by my side.

Brady glanced over at her but only for a second. He was focused on me. He wouldn't know what to say to me. I knew that, because if the situations were reversed, I wouldn't know what to say to him, either.

"You okay?" he asked, watching me cautiously. Like I would break down at any moment. Didn't he get that I'd been dealing with this for a long time now?

"Yeah," I replied, which was a lie, but I wasn't going to make him feel any worse.

He let out a heavy sigh and ran his hand through his hair as he stared off across the street. He was thinking. He wanted me to tell him. I knew that. But what was he going to do once I did? Tell me he was sorry? That he was here for me if I needed him? Didn't he know how pointless those words were? He couldn't do anything for me. He couldn't make this better.

"He's been sick for about eighteen months," I finally said, knowing it was the right thing to do. "The past couple months he's gotten really bad. Doctors sent him home because there's nothing else that can be done."

Brady closed his eyes tightly and inhaled sharply through his nose. I waited for him to speak. I wasn't sure I could tell him anything more. I didn't want to talk about it.

When he opened his eyes, he looked at me. "Why didn't

you tell us . . . or me at least? This isn't something you have to go through alone. We'd have been there for you."

I felt Maggie's fingers gently brush against my hand. She was silently trying to encourage me.

"I didn't want to accept it or talk about it. Telling y'all made it real. I needed to keep going like it wasn't real. But now . . . I can't keep doing that. Things aren't good. It's bad now," I explained.

He needed to understand why I'd left him in the dark about something so major in my life. He'd been my best friend since we were six. I knew he didn't understand this and my not telling him. But it was how I needed to cope.

"What can I do?" Brady asked, looking pained.

Before there wasn't anything he could do. But now he was standing between something . . . or someone I needed. Someone who could help me.

"Let me be friends with Maggie. Just friends. She's helped me in ways no one else could."

I glanced over at her and saw her eyes had gone wide. She hadn't expected that. It made her gorgeous face cute. For the first time in a long time I felt like laughing.

"You want to be friends with Maggie?" Brady asked, sounding confused. "I don't understand."

He wouldn't. But she didn't talk to him. He didn't know how the sound of her voice could soothe an ache.

He didn't know having someone to talk to who understood the pain I was going through was exactly what I needed. I didn't need to talk to him or any of the guys. They didn't get it. Only Maggie.

Then You Shouldn't Be So Damn Pretty

CHAPTER 13

MAGGIE

I watched Brady's face as he stood there staring at me, then staring at West as if he hadn't heard him correctly. I had to admit, I was just as surprised. West wanted to be my friend. Because I helped him. Like no one else could.

My chest felt warm, and there was a funny flutter in my stomach.

"You wouldn't understand. No one does. Except for Maggie. She's helped me a lot the past few days. Having her to talk to is what I need right now."

The flutter turned into birds flapping around in my stomach. I had to remember West had said, "Just friends." He hadn't said, *I'd like to kiss her again.*

He was hurting, and he liked talking to me. That was all this was.

"She . . . uh . . . she doesn't talk," Brady said, glancing at me with an apologetic look on his face.

I waited. I didn't want West to tell Brady that I talked to him. But then how else did he explain wanting to be my friend?

"She has her own way of communicating, and that's enough," West replied.

I wanted to sigh in relief. If my aunt Coralee knew I was talking to West, she'd be trying to get me to talk to her.

Brady pressed his lips together then nodded. "Okay. Yeah . . . if you want to be friends I'm okay with that. But just friends. Don't—" He paused, and I felt West tense beside me.

"She's safe with me. I respect her, and I also won't let anyone else hurt her," West said with firm determination in his voice.

The birds in my stomach started up again. He wanted to be friends. I could do that. I wanted that. I needed that too.

Brady appeared to believe him. "Good. Well, you want to come inside? Mom made chocolate cake."

"Yeah." West looked down at me. "You like chocolate cake?"

I hesitated then nodded. I didn't want to interfere in Brady's life, but West wanted me there, and I wanted to be there for him. This side of West wasn't anything like I expected. He wasn't cruel or hard. He wasn't putting up a façade for anyone. This was the guy I wanted him to be when he kissed me that time at the field.

"Then let's go get a slice of Coralee's. It's delicious."

Brady looked confused, but he turned and headed inside. West nodded for me to follow Brady, and as I did, West fell into step beside me.

I could eat some cake with West then go up to my room and leave Brady alone with his friends. That way I made both boys happy while still protecting myself. No matter how much I wanted to be there to help West because I knew what it was like to do this alone, I wouldn't let my guard down completely.

Brady walked inside and headed for the den. Aunt Coralee stepped into the hallway from the kitchen and smiled when she saw West. It was a sad smile but also one that said she was happy to see him. I knew she was worried about him.

"West, sweetheart, it's so good to see you. I missed you this summer. You're not around enough." She went straight to him and hugged him, then pulled back and looked at me. "You're back from your walk," she said, sounding pleased.

"Now you've burned some calories, you want to have a slice of chocolate cake with me in the kitchen?"

"She's actually going to go have some cake in the den with us," Brady informed his mother.

Aunt Coralee's eyes went wide, then she smiled brightly. "Well, okay. That's wonderful. I'll bring some fresh milk and two more glasses in there." She turned and hurried back to the kitchen.

"I think that just made her day," Brady whispered, glancing back at me.

And this time I smiled. Because he was right. She was happy, and that made me smile.

West's hand slid behind my back, and he led me into the den where the guys I was used to seeing around Brady were lounging on sofas and beanbags, while a couple were shooting hoops at a basketball hoop on the wall.

"Maggie!" Nash said the moment he turned around from taking a shot and saw me standing there. It was the first time he'd spoken to me since I'd sent him that text. I guess the shock of seeing me in here made him forget he was ignoring me.

West kept his hand on my back as he moved me into the room toward the table.

It was obvious Brady hadn't told the other guys about West's dad. None of them looked at him like they were worried about him or like they didn't know what to do. I was relieved for him. He had just faced Brady and Aunt Coralee. He needed a break before he faced the rest of them.

"So, Maggie's here . . . with West," Nash said because no one else was saying anything.

Brady turned and looked at all of them. "Maggie and West are friends. Just friends. And I'm good with that."

There was an awkward silence, and West pulled out a chair for me to sit. Once I was seated he looked at his friends and teammates who were still watching the three of us like they weren't sure what to think.

"She's my friend. Deal with it," he informed them, then sat down close to me. He leaned his head toward mine. "Sorry they're acting like idiots. I don't normally have girls who are friends. And you were completely off-limits because of Brady. So they're trying to figure out what's up."

I nodded. I understood that. Although right now all I really wanted was to run off to my room.

"Here's more milk and cake," Aunt Coralee announced.

The guys went back to watching TV and talking. I didn't turn around to see if Nash was still playing basketball or staring at us.

"She doesn't eat enough. Make sure she finishes the whole thing," she told West as if she knew we were friends now and the idea tickled her pink.

"Yes, ma'am," he replied, taking the plates from her hands and putting one in front of me.

When she left the room, West smiled down at me. "You need to relax. You look like I'm forcing you to sit here beside me. They'll get over it soon enough. I swear."

I tilted my head down to hide my mouth from everyone else. "I know," I replied quietly. "I just hate being stared at."

He chuckled and moved his fork to get a bite of cake. "Then you shouldn't be so damn pretty."

The birds in my stomach were back. How was I supposed to eat now?

Do You Have Regrets?

CHAPTER 14

WEST

Maggie had slipped off to her room when we started watching last week's game tape. I had been so relaxed watching the plays and talking about where we messed up and where we needed to tighten up that I missed her leaving.

I hadn't gone after her—I knew she had wanted to escape. I could tell by the look on her face. She'd only been staying for me.

But now my head wasn't on the game anymore. I was thinking about my dad and the fact I'd been gone too long. I wanted to get back home and check on things. Talk to him even if he didn't talk back. I'd found that didn't matter anymore. I just needed to be near him.

The end was coming, and it wasn't going to be easy.

I stood up and walked over to Brady and then whispered I was heading home and told him to text me Maggie's phone number. The guys were so wrapped up in watching the game, they didn't notice or say anything about me heading out early.

I wasn't in my truck yet when my phone dinged. Brady had sent me her number. I'd almost expected him to tell me to get it from her myself. But he trusted me with her. I'd make sure I deserved that trust.

It helped just knowing I could call and hear her voice if I needed to. And I wondered if the sound of my voice helped *her*? She'd been through something virtually alone. Could I be for her what she was for me?

I opened the truck door and glanced up at her window. She was sitting in the window seat, her knees tucked up under her chin, watching me. I lifted my hand to wave, and she did the same. Then I held up my phone and put it to my ear and pointed at her.

Just to be sure she understood, I quickly texted her.

It's me. Brady gave me your number. If I call, will you answer?

I pressed send then looked back up at her. She glanced down at her phone and I watched as she typed something. When her face lifted again to look down at me, my phone dinged.

Yes. If you need me, I'll answer.

That was enough. I nodded and climbed into the truck to drive home and face my reality. I would sit and talk to Dad. I'd tell him about watching the game with the guys. And I'd tell him about Maggie. He'd like her.

When I opened the door to the house, it was quiet. The hospice worker was gone for the day. I locked up and headed inside. There was a note on the table from Momma telling me that she had made me a sub sandwich and left it in the fridge along with a fresh gallon of sweet tea. Dad had asked for her, so she had gone to lie down beside him.

I wasn't hungry. I'd eaten two slices of cake earlier, and now knowing I wouldn't get to talk to Dad tonight, I didn't feel much like eating. But Momma would worry if she checked the fridge in the morning and saw the sandwich still there. So I fixed a tall glass of iced tea and took the sandwich and drink with me up to my room. I'd try to eat some before I went to sleep. If not, I'd make sure she never saw it wasn't eaten.

I set my food down then walked quietly up the hall to stand outside my parents' bedroom door and listen. There was silence. My dad used to snore, but he never did that anymore. He slept so quietly now. I used to lie in my bed at night, covering my ears, wanting him to stop snoring so I could fall asleep. These days I found myself wishing for his snoring. Just so I'd know he was still breathing.

My heart clenched at the idea of my dad no longer breathing. The panic and pain that came with that thought squeezed my throat, making it hard to inhale. I moved away from their door and went back to my room so I didn't disturb my mother. Closing my door behind me, I placed both hands on the door to hold myself up as I hung my head and gasped for air.

I was going to lose him.

I knew that, but damn, it hurt so bad.

Every time I let the facts sink in, my emotions began to lose their grip. I felt my body tremble as tears blurred my eyes. How was I going to make it through life without my dad? I needed him. We needed him.

I managed to inhale sharply, and I coughed to clear my throat before pushing off from the door and walking over to my bed to sink down onto it. My phone pressed against my leg where I'd stuck it into my pocket.

Maggie's face entered my thoughts, and without thinking about it, I pulled my phone out and scanned the contacts for her number.

She answered on the second ring.

"Hello," she said softly.

It was late, but I knew the guys wouldn't have left Brady's yet.

"Were you asleep?" I asked.

"No. I'm still sitting right where you saw me last," she replied.

I closed my eyes and pictured her up there in that window. Lost in her thoughts. In her solitude. She had spent so much time the past two years locked inside herself. Not talking to others. I didn't like to think about it. The idea of her being alone hurt me. I understood it, but I wished I'd been able to be there for her the way she was for me. Maybe now I could be that friend she needed. Just like she was mine.

"Did you ever have times when you couldn't breathe? When the pain was so intense, it squeezed your throat and held on tight?"

"Yes. It's called a panic attack. I had them a lot. I haven't since I moved here, though."

So I wasn't losing my mind. This was normal. "How did you deal with them?"

She sighed. "I didn't at first. Once, I even passed out from not breathing. But I learned to think about something that made me happy. That gave me peace. I refused to let the pain control me. And the squeezing would ease up, and I could breathe again."

She gave me peace. She was the only thing that had given me peace in a long time.

"Are you afraid to close your eyes at night?" I asked her.

"Yes. Because I know the nightmare will come. It always does."

"Me too. I'm afraid he won't wake up tomorrow," I replied.

She was quiet for a moment. We both sat there and listened to the other breathe. Oddly, it was enough.

"One day that is what will happen, West. And it will be incredibly hard. But what you can do now is make the most out of the time you have left. Talk to him even if he can't talk back. Hold his hand. Tell him everything you want him to know. So when he's gone you don't have regrets."

Her mother had been taken from her without warning. And so had her father with his horrible, sick act. She'd lost it all just like that. She was right. I had time to make sure I didn't have regrets.

"Do you have regrets?" I asked, already knowing the answer. I could hear it in her voice.

"Yes. So many," was her soft reply.

I couldn't imagine sweet Maggie having anything to regret. She was kind and gentle. It was hard to think of her being anything less than perfect.

"I'm sure you were the daughter every mother wanted," I assured her. "I know yours had to have been very proud of you."

She didn't reply at first, and I was afraid I was making her talk about it too much. I had been focusing on her pain to forget mine. I hadn't been careful enough.

"Two hours before my mother died, I told her she was ruining my life," Maggie said, then let out a bitter laugh. "Because I wanted to go to a party that my friend was having at her house, and my mother didn't feel like there was proper adult supervision there. I wanted to go so bad. I had thought her not letting me go was the end of the world. The worst thing that could happen to me. If I had only known two hours later that I'd lose her . . . that I would find out what the worst thing that could ever happen to me truly felt like."

I closed my eyes and felt her regret heavy inside me as if it were my own. She had been a fifteen-year-old girl wanting to grow up. She had been acting out like all teenagers did. Hell, I had my fair share of screw-ups. It was just so fucking unfair that she'd lost her mother that way before she could fix it. Before she could apologize and make it right.

"She knew you didn't mean it," I told her, feeling like the words were inadequate. But I didn't know what else to say.

"I hope so. But it will always be my biggest regret," she replied.

I Was a Liar. Fantastic.
CHAPTER 15

MAGGIE

I woke up with my phone on my pillow. Then I had lain there and just stared at it for several minutes. I'd talked to West for more than three hours last night. Until I'd fallen asleep. Hearing my own voice when I knew he needed me to talk to him wasn't hard. Yet the idea of speaking to someone else terrified me.

For so long I'd thought hearing my voice again would send me back into the corner, screaming uncontrollably. But it wasn't doing that. I was talking to West with ease. Last night I had actually talked about things I'd thought I never wanted to talk about again. And I hadn't had a panic attack or curled up into a ball and whimpered.

But was I ready to talk to other people?

No. I'd given them the only words I was going to give them.

I didn't want them asking me things like West had. I didn't want them making me speak in a courtroom where I would have to face my father. The man who had never missed seeing me cheer. Who'd clapped the loudest at my school play when I'd walked out as a bear instead of Goldilocks, which was who I'd really wanted to be. Who'd sung "Happy Birthday" to me dressed in a Superman costume with my Marvel comics cake in his hands the year I was obsessed with superheroes. That man was dead to me now. He had made every good memory a bad one. He had become something else. Someone else. Someone I couldn't talk about or see.

If I talked, they'd want me to talk about him. About what I saw him do. About how he begged me to forgive him as I screamed for my mother to wake up. And I couldn't do that. I wasn't ready. I doubted I ever would be. I had watched him verbally and sometimes physically abuse my mother most of my life. Then he'd buy her jewelry or flowers and tell both of us over and over how much he adored us. Remembering the way he would refer to us as "my girls" made my stomach churn.

Climbing out of bed, I began to get dressed and put

those memories that were threatening to break through back in the tightly shut box I kept them in.

Brady parked the truck in front of school, but instead of getting right out, he looked over at me. I'd been lost in my thoughts all morning.

"West has been my best friend since we were little kids. I love him like a brother. I hate that he's gone through all this with his dad alone, but it's also so like him. He doesn't let people get too close. He's never been one to trust people. He always trusted me, though. Until this." He paused and sighed heavily. "He's decided to trust you. I think he's being honest about wanting to just be your friend. But I also worry about you getting attached to him. You've been through your own pain, Maggie. I don't want him to use you. He won't mean to, but I'm afraid he will. Please guard yourself. Understand he needs you right now. Maybe having someone to talk to that doesn't talk back is what he needs, and you fit that bill. But just don't let him hurt you. Okay?"

I thought about my attraction to West. He was hard not to be attracted to. But I wasn't going to take his need to have someone who understood the pain of losing a parent as something more. I knew he didn't look at me that way. Heck, he didn't even act like we'd ever kissed. It had been no big deal to him, and I had forgiven him for the harsh

cruelty I'd seen in him before. I understood he'd been acting out because he was hurting. He pushed everyone away.
But he wasn't pushing me away anymore, and now it was
hard to remember to keep him at arm's length.

I just nodded. I appreciated that Brady was trying to
protect me.

He reached for the truck door and opened it. That was
the end of this conversation. I grabbed my book bag and
headed into school.

I would be lying to myself if I said my stomach wasn't
all fluttery about getting to see West. Last night had been as
special as it had been difficult. Even after Brady gave me a
warning I really needed to listen to, I couldn't help but feel
very giddy about being near West. Having him look at me
and talk to me.

When I saw our lockers, I paused. The giddiness and
fluttery feeling in my stomach was snatched away instantly.
West was there, but so was some girl. She was a cheerleader.
I knew that from watching her at the pep rally. Her long
blond hair was curled and styled to perfection as she bit her
bottom lip and batted her eyes up at West. Then there was
the way West was looking at her. The way he never looked
at me. Like he wanted to eat her up.

My stomach twisted, and my throat tightened. The girl
put her hand on his chest and he reached up and covered it

with his own. Then he winked at her. That was enough for me. I would just carry all my books to first period, and I'd make do with one of my other notebooks.

I hurried to class, trying not to think about my reaction to seeing West and another girl. Sure, I had seen him with Raleigh a bunch of times. But this time it hurt more. I was being unfair and probably ridiculous, because as West's friend I should be glad he was smiling and winking at a girl rather than being sad. But as the girl currently secretly crushing on West, I was a little cracked around the edges.

Brady's words came back to me as I sat down at an empty desk. I needed to be careful. West just wanted my friendship. No more thinking about him any other way. And I had to find the off switch to the flutters in my stomach. Maybe the blonde was just the off switch I needed.

Mr. Trout came in the room, and everyone who was still standing around outside in the halls began to file into the classroom. Gunner Lawton, one of Brady's friends, came in last, along with Ryker Lee. Ryker glanced over at me and smiled before heading to the back of the class to sit beside Gunner. The football players always stayed together.

Next class I had to face Charlie. After yesterday's lunch fiasco, I wasn't sure I wanted to do that. But I didn't have a choice. At least in this class no one ever spoke to me or acknowledged me. Mr. Trout was one of the teachers who thought he needed to yell so I could hear him. I always did my best not to draw attention to myself so he wouldn't try to tell me something.

My phone vibrated in my pocket. I continued to get my notebook and textbook ready for the lecture when it vibrated again. After checking to make sure Mr. Trout was still eating his breakfast and reading the newspaper at his desk, I pulled my phone out to check to see who it was. I didn't normally get texts at school. The last time had been when Nash was trying to talk to me.

I didn't see you at your locker this morning. Brady said you were here. You okay?

It was from West. He wouldn't have noticed me at my locker this morning. He'd been too wrapped up in that cheerleader. Dang it, I was doing it again. I couldn't be this way if we were going to be friends. He needed a friend. But this was so hard. I hadn't imagined being West Ashby's friend would be this difficult. Why I hadn't thought this all through, I don't know. I knew how he was. I knew how he acted out to deal with his inner turmoil. But still . . . this wasn't easy.

I'm here. I didn't need anything from my locker, so I came on to first period so I would have a chance to go over my homework.

Now I was a liar. Fantastic.

I slipped the phone back into my pocket before I got

caught, and made a mental list of things I should work on. Things that had nothing to do with West. Like I should start practicing the piano again. My mother used to love hearing me play. She would have wanted me to keep playing.

By the time Mr. Trout had polished off his Egg McMuffin and drunk his coffee, I was in a better place. I had goals, and I was not going to get attached to West Ashby.

She Didn't Belong to Me

CHAPTER 16

WEST

When first period was over, I headed straight to my locker to wait on Maggie. Not seeing her this morning had made me edgy. I should probably get a grip on my need to have her around, but right now I had too much other shit to deal with. I was attached to her. It wasn't a bad thing.

As I walked down the hallway, an arm wrapped around mine, and I felt tits press into my arm. I knew it was Serena before I even glanced down at her. She was determined to move in on me now that it was really over with Raleigh. Serena and Raleigh had been competing with each other for as long as I could remember.

When Serena had met me at my locker this morning, I

had considered letting her distract me. She was sexy as hell, and all that blond hair was hot. But in the ten minutes she'd flirted with me at my locker, she'd already started getting on my nerves. Her voice was too high-pitched, and she batted her eyelashes so damn much, I was afraid they'd come off because those jokers were too long to be real.

"We have next period together. Sit by me. I'll make class so much more enjoyable," she said as she leaned into me.

I knew the kinds of things Serena did in class to make it more enjoyable. I'd seen it in action more than once. But I wasn't feeling it. Not today. I just needed to see Maggie.

"I'm sure you could," I replied. I wasn't going to be mean. I just needed to get her to back off.

She giggled and held on to me tighter. It was making me feel claustrophobic. I didn't like the feeling of not being able to take a deep breath. And where was Maggie?

I scanned the crowd as I walked to our lockers. Serena was talking, but I wasn't listening anymore. Maggie wasn't at her locker again, and my edginess was getting worse.

I stopped and looked back to see if she was anywhere in this hallway. But no sign of her. "Who you looking for?" Serena asked, still locked on to me.

I wasn't telling her. She'd be on Maggie fast. I knew how girls like Serena worked. She'd make sure Maggie understood she was claiming me, and sweet Maggie couldn't say a word back to her. Serena didn't understand guy-and-girl friendships. She'd assume I was moving in on Maggie. Not that the idea of kissing Maggie again and holding her didn't appeal to me . . . I thought about it often enough. It was just that I wasn't good enough for what Maggie needed. I couldn't be that guy. I didn't do relationships well, and Maggie deserved the best.

But I could be one hell of a friend.

Glancing back at the locker and seeing there was still no Maggie, I shook Serena loose. "I gotta go. I need to do something. I won't be in next period," I said distractedly as I kept searching the halls. Then I moved toward Brady's next class, because he'd know where I could find her. It wasn't like Maggie not to go to her locker. What was she doing? Just carrying all her books around today?

As soon as I turned the corner, my eyes locked on her. She was bent over by the far wall, pulling books out of her overstuffed book bag. My relief at just seeing her should worry me. I'd started needing her too much.

For the first time all day a smile pulled at my lips.

She was biting her bottom lip, and a frustrated frown was wrinkling her brow. She let out a huff and stood up to tuck the hair that had fallen in her face behind her ear. Just as she slipped the strands back and sighed, her eyes found mine.

Her eyes briefly flashed with happiness and only made my smile bigger. But then she shut it down fast and gave me a tight smile before bending back over her book bag and quickly jamming all the books she'd just taken out back in. What was the girl doing?

I made my way over to her and dropped to my haunches until we were at eye level. I watched her study my feet for a moment before she slowly lifted her gaze to meet mine. Her cheeks turned pink.

"They have these things called lockers. It keeps us from having to carry around a shit ton of books all day. You should check yours out," I teased, wanting that tight fake smile to become a real one.

Was she feeling weird about us talking until we'd fallen asleep last night? I couldn't figure out how the girl I'd gone to sleep talking to was now avoiding me. Because now that I'd found her and saw the way she was trying not to look at me, I knew she hadn't come to her locker because of me.

"Seriously, Maggie, let me take this bag to your locker and unload this stuff. It's too heavy for you to be carrying around. I'm gonna have to take you to my chiropractor if you do this all day."

She zipped up her bag and then stood up. I did the same. But before she could pick up her bag, I grabbed it.

"Come on," I said, putting my hand on her lower back and moving her through the crowd toward our lockers.

She let me guide her, and I liked the way it felt to put my hand on her this way. I'd put my hand there on other girls before, but it had never felt like this. Almost as if I were making sure everyone knew Maggie was mine. Which was ridiculous, because she wasn't *mine*; she was my friend. She didn't belong to me.

Though, the idea of her being mine apparently appealed to me enough to make my heart speed up thinking about it. But *no*. I had to shut this down. I was emotional and messed up. Maggie was my peace in the storm. I couldn't confuse that with something else and ruin everything.

I had her combination memorized from helping her last week. I'd committed it to memory without even realizing it. I got her locker open quickly, then started filling it with the books from her bag. "Which ones do you need to keep out?" I asked, glancing back at her.

She stepped closer to me, and the scent of vanilla came with her. I didn't move. I stayed where I was and inhaled. There was no perfume smell. Just . . . Maggie.

Maggie took a textbook from her locker and reached into the book bag I was holding. She took out a notebook then stepped back. Her smell lingered, and I finished putting her book bag away while telling myself I had to draw a line with her. Wanting to take a sniff every time I was near her was not going to be cool.

Once I had her books in there, I closed her locker and turned back to her. "You gonna tell me why you didn't come to your locker this morning?" Still not sure if she'd talk to me here. Where people could see.

She ducked her head and reached for her book bag. When she finally looked back up at me, she shrugged.

She wasn't talking.

That was okay. If she just wanted to talk to me when we were alone, I could deal with that. I'd just need to be alone with her more. Which, given how much it appealed to me, might prove difficult. Knowing how her lips felt and trying to get close enough to inhale her scent were two reasons that being alone with Maggie wasn't going to be easy.

Shit. I had to get a grip. Maybe Serena was a good thing. She knew the score. She wasn't in it for anything more than sex and bragging rights.

I reached over and tucked the lock of hair that had gotten loose back behind her ear. It only teased me. When I looked at her or touched her, it was hard to want someone else.

"I missed you this morning. I look forward to seeing you at the lockers. When you didn't come, it messed with my head," I explained.

A new softness in her expression transformed her face back to the Maggie from last night. The one who trusted me. I liked that look.

She took a step toward me, and her hand gently brushed mine, not once but twice, before she smiled up at me. My chest tightened. Then she turned and walked away.

West Was Showing Me I Wasn't Broken
CHAPTER 17

MAGGIE

I was sunk. This thing I felt for West had vaulted right over the crush I was afraid of and gone straight to full-blown feelings for him. He was being too sweet. How was I supposed to deal with not getting attached to West Ashby when he was being so dang nice?

He hadn't been at our lockers after second period, but he rarely ever was. His classes were on the other side of the building, and coming back in between would make him late for class. I didn't go to my own locker between third and fourth periods for the very same reason.

So it was lunchtime before I saw him again. Walking into the cafeteria, I let my gaze go directly to his table. I had to remind myself he was just my friend when I saw the blond cheerleader beside him. He liked her. It was obvious. He liked her the way he didn't like me. My flutters weren't there now; they were more like an ache in my chest.

Maybe if West hadn't kissed me, if I didn't have to face the fact he'd tried me out and not liked me that way, it would be easier to deal with this. But when I saw him with another girl, it served as a reminder that I hadn't been to his liking. Plain and simple, he just wanted me as a friend because I understood what it was like to lose your parents and still survive.

His eyes moved away from the girl and locked on mine. Then he winked. God, why did he have to wink at me? I forced a smile I hoped looked real and moved to get into the food line. Charlie hadn't talked to me in second or fourth period today. He'd smiled at me awkwardly, but that had been it. So I figured he wouldn't show up in line and ask me to sit with him today.

All I could do was listen to the conversations around me. I found out from the girls in front of me, who kept looking at West's table, that the girl was Serena. Everyone expected her to be the girl West moved on to after Raleigh. I also overheard that Raleigh had been in the bathroom crying over Serena and West this morning.

I genuinely felt bad for her. It had to be hard to lose West Ashby.

By the time I got my tray, I'd also learned that Serena and Raleigh were archrivals. So this was probably going to end up in a catfight in the hallway. . . .

I didn't even glance at West's table when I went to go find a seat. I wasn't going to be pathetic, looking like I was hoping for him to invite me over. Truth was, that was the last thing I wanted. Watching him and Serena while I ate didn't seem appealing at all. So I made my way to the back doors and went to sit outside at one of the picnic tables.

This wasn't a popular place to eat. It was hot out. Alabama didn't start to cool down until October. Everyone seemed to want to stay in the air-conditioned cafeteria. Only the loners made their way out here. I was a loner, so this fit me. Although when it got colder, I wasn't sure I'd be able to stick it out.

There were five picnic tables outside, and four of them had one person each sitting at them. And on the patch of grass underneath each of the two large oak trees was a student with a sandwich in one hand and a book in the other. This seemed to be my place. I went to the one empty table and set my tray down. Then I pulled out the library book I had stuck in my bag. I could read while I ate.

"What're you doing out here? It's ninety degrees,

Maggie." West's voice startled me, and I jerked my gaze up from my book to see him standing on the other side of the table.

He was so tall. Especially when I was sitting down. He had his arms crossed over his wide chest, and his jeans hung low on his hips. The snug-fit T-shirt he was wearing did little to hide all the wonder that was West's body.

I just stared at him. I wasn't going to answer. He should know that by now.

"Come inside. We have room at our table," he said, nodding back toward the door.

I wasn't going in there to eat with him and Serena. No way. It may be childish, but I wasn't ready to watch that. I shook my head.

He frowned, and a crease formed between his brows. "Why not?"

I shrugged and dropped my gaze back down to my tray of untouched food.

"Please? If you don't come in there, I'm coming out here, and I really fucking hate to eat in the heat."

I lifted my eyes back to meet his, and this time I frowned. Why would he come out here? I was fine. I had a book. No one at that table wanted me there. Especially Brady. I held up my book to show him, and then I put it back down.

He chuckled, and my stomach fluttered. Dang it.

"You want to read in the heat instead of sitting inside with me?"

I nodded.

"That's a blow to my ego, babe."

Babe. He'd just called me babe. Of course I'd also heard him call other girls babe. But he'd never called me that. I would not smile like an idiot. *Babe* wasn't even a very nice word. I should be insulted.

But I wasn't insulted at all. Crap.

"Are you worried about Brady? Because he's fine with our friendship. I've even got Serena in there too. He sees that. He knows I'm not moving in on you."

That got me back to where I needed to be. Thank you, West Ashby, for reminding me where I stood. I really wanted to read my book. I held it up again and gave him a tight smile.

He frowned and let out a frustrated sigh. "Fine, read your book."

I nodded in agreement. That was exactly what I'd planned to do. He shook his head and turned and left me there. Alone again. Just like I'd asked for.

Good.

Well, it was supposed to be good. It was what I wanted.

So why did it feel even lonelier now that he was gone? If he'd just stayed inside and not come out here, I would have been perfectly content. Now I was going to have a hard time concentrating on my book.

I saw West again at my locker before last period. He said he hoped I enjoyed my book. Then he brushed the hair off my shoulder before leaving me.

Aunt Coralee picked me up from school like she usually did, since Brady had football practice for three hours every day. She always had a snack waiting for me when I got home, and she chatted about her day.

I listened while I ate, and when she asked me questions, I answered with a nod. She didn't expect more and, unlike Jorie, she didn't seem annoyed when I didn't reply. My godmother still hadn't texted me to see how I was. I'd kind of expected her to. It wasn't that I missed her—being away from her was definitely a relief—but she'd still been a big part of my life growing up. She was like my aunt. Always at family events and holidays.

Once I was done eating, I hugged Aunt Coralee because she liked it when I did that, and then I headed upstairs to my room. Uncle Boone wouldn't be home for a few more hours. He would get off work and then go to Brady's practice and watch the last of it. Then they'd talk about it over dinner. Like they did every night.

I knew the routine here, and I felt comfortable with it.

I wondered whether, if I'd come to live here right after my mother's death, I'd be better by now. If I would trust people more. Maybe I would be different. Maybe I wouldn't have lost so much of myself. Wouldn't have lost the girl I'd once been. I didn't know her at all anymore.

I no longer heard from the friends I used to have. They stopped texting me weeks after everything happened. Mostly because I never responded. My best friend and my boyfriend had gone to prom together that year. I'd seen their photos on Instagram. I hadn't even cared. None of that had mattered anymore.

And I had thought that nothing would matter again. That I'd lost all those emotions and feelings. But West was showing me that I wasn't broken. That my heart still worked and I still could care. I just wished it wasn't all working and caring for him.

I fell back on my bed and stared at the ceiling. I needed to get myself level-headed again. West was watching his father die. I knew how painful that was. He needed me to be his friend. He had enough girls wanting him for something more. He didn't need that from me, too. So pouting and getting upset over him and a girl was wrong. If a girl made him smile, I should be thankful for that.

I was going to be a friend to West. I wouldn't let my heart keep me from being what he needed.

We Weren't That Damn Funny
CHAPTER 18

WEST

It was game day. I used to love Fridays during football season. Dad would always wake me up, and we'd eat breakfast together while we talked over the plays and what I needed to do to win.

This morning I'd woken up to a clatter of dishes in the kitchen. I'd jumped up and run down the hall to find Momma standing in the middle of a pile of broken plates. Tears had been streaming down her face as she'd looked up at me. "I was trying"—she'd sniffed—"to make you break-fast. I couldn't reach the top shelf. Your dad always reached the waffle iron for me. I slipped and pulled the second shelf down with me." Another sob had shaken her chest.

I'd gone over to her and pulled her into a hug. "Momma, go back in there and be with Dad. I can make my own breakfast. I'll clean all this up. He needs you with him."

She'd nodded against my chest and sobbed again.

That was how I'd started my day.

Getting to school and seeing Maggie was all I thought about as I kissed Mom's cheek good-bye and then kissed my dad's forehead and promised him we'd win big tonight. I'd tell him all about it when I got home.

My chest hurt, and my throat felt tight, but I knew if I could see Maggie, if I could hear her voice, I'd be okay. Calling her wasn't an option because she'd be in Brady's truck and she wouldn't talk in front of him. So I had to get to her this morning and get her alone. Before I completely broke down.

Brady's truck was parked outside school when I pulled up. Never had I been more thankful to see it in my life. I didn't waste any time talking to people who called out my name. I had to get to my locker. To Maggie.

When I saw the back of her hair, my chest eased some. She was here. I focused on her as I made my way through the crowd, needing to remind myself that I could do this. I could make it through this. Maggie was with me.

"Hey," I said almost breathlessly as I got to our lockers. I waited for her to turn and look at me. It was odd how just the promise of seeing her made things seem better.

She closed her locker and then turned to face me. The smile on her lips slowly fell as she studied my face. She knew. Without me saying a word, she knew I was dealing with some shit. That was something I needed from her. Her understanding without me having to explain.

Her hand slid over mine as she stared up at me with a gentle strength that was just *Maggie*. I flipped my hand over and threaded my fingers through hers. Then she squeezed my hand tightly even though it dwarfed her small one. "I'm here," she whispered, barely moving her lips.

That was what I needed. The tightness in my chest eased away, and I could breathe deeply again. "Bad morning," I explained, although she'd already figured that out.

She nodded and her thumb brushed against my hand. I liked the way it felt to have her palm pressed against mine. Everything I doubted about myself, about my ability to deal with this, about life—she cleared it all away with just one touch.

"Good morning, sexy." Serena's voice broke the spell that had been wrapping around us, and Maggie's hand was instantly gone. She moved away from me before I could say anything, and then she slipped past me and into the crowd.

I jerked away from Serena's hand on my shoulder, pissed she'd interrupted us. I didn't get much time with

Maggie during the day. If I was going to play tonight, I needed her to help get my head right.

"What's wrong? You tense about tonight? You know you'll be amazing. You always are."

I moved to my locker without answering her. The past couple of days she'd been good for me. With her hands on me and her mouth doing things for me that felt more than good, I wasn't thinking about anything else.

But today Serena would have to back off. Sex was not what I needed. Forgetting everything by getting off between her legs or in her mouth wouldn't work today. That only lasted for a few minutes. Then the shit was all back.

Only Maggie's presence helped me.

"What's the matter? You're all grumpy. Come to the bathroom and I'll ease some tension for you. Like yesterday. You liked that, didn't you?"

I didn't want to be reminded how low I had sunk. If Maggie knew I used girls like this, she'd be disgusted with me. She hadn't used anyone to ease her pain. She'd dealt with it alone.

No one got hurt just so she could feel better.

"Not interested today. I got the game to focus on," I finally said to Serena, moving past her and toward my first-period class before she could catch up to me.

*   *   *

By lunchtime I had missed Maggie at her locker twice more, thanks to Serena holding me up in the hallway. My gaze was locked on the door of the cafeteria, waiting on Maggie to come inside. I knew she'd go out to the picnic tables again. She'd been doing that most of the week. I'd tried to get her to come inside, but she didn't want to. She wanted to sit in the heat and read.

Serena came in first and made her way straight toward me. I knew I'd asked for this by messing around with her, but today I wanted her to just step back. We were fooling around; we weren't in a relationship. She seemed to be forgetting that, even though I'd made it very clear before we had sex the first time on Wednesday. Two days later does not make us exclusive.

But she sure was trying to get her claws in me.

I shifted my gaze back to the door, waiting on Maggie. Just seeing her would help.

"So, you and Serena, huh?" Brady asked as he sat down across from me.

I shrugged. "Not serious."

He laughed while opening his drink. "I don't think she realizes that."

"I made it clear Wednesday when she started this thing."

Brady nodded. "You fuck her?"

This wasn't his business, but I nodded.

He smirked. "Actions speak louder than words."

I was getting pissed. What was his deal? It wasn't like he wasn't fucking Ivy, and we all knew he wasn't serious about her. She was a rebound from that mystery girl he'd dated this summer. The one he was always too busy with to do anything else. The one none of us had ever met.

"What's your problem?" I asked, annoyed, and still keeping one eye on the door for Maggie.

He leaned forward. "My problem is, you're going through hell right now. I want to help you, but I don't know how. The person you want to help you has been through her own hell, and she doesn't need you holding her hand secretly in the halls and fucking Serena in the damn bathroom hours later."

Whoa. Okay, so he saw us holding hands this morning. That was what this was about. I got that.

"You're my best friend, West. I can't imagine what you are dealing with. But I do know Maggie doesn't need you playing with her head. It's not fair to use her, man. She lost both parents at once. In a fucked-up, crazy, horrific way. Don't do this to her. Please, don't hurt her."

Serena sat down beside me before I could say anything else. "Y'all ready for the game tonight?" she asked in true cheerleader-pep style.

Brady glanced at her and gave her a smile that didn't

meet his eyes and nodded before dropping his gaze to his food.

I wasn't hurting Maggie. It wasn't like she had feelings for me in that way. I had been careful to keep this at a friends level. I mean, she hadn't even liked me in the beginning. She understood me now, but she wasn't attached to me. Was she? No, she wasn't. She was too good for me, and deep down she knew it. I had explained to Brady that we were just friends. So, obviously, I was allowed to fuck other girls. And I wouldn't hurt Maggie. Hell, I'd kill anyone who did.

Serena was saying something, but I didn't hear her because Maggie had walked into the cafeteria. Her gaze immediately locked on mine. She smiled at me then turned away quickly. Like she did every day. She wouldn't look at me long, and that smile wasn't a real one. Why wouldn't she look at me? Had I done something wrong?

Asa sat down on my left, and Gunner sat down beside Brady. Talk about tonight's game soon took over, and I didn't let myself worry about Maggie sitting outside all alone, reading in the fucking sun. I also managed to ignore Serena's annoying laughter. We weren't that damn funny. Why did she laugh so much?

CHAPTER 19

MAGGIE

I need to talk to you.

I stared down at my phone. It was a text from West. He'd been upset this morning, but I left when Serena showed up. I wasn't into watching them be all over each other. I was doing what I promised myself, and being his friend. That didn't mean I had to like Serena.

Thursday I'd ended up in the restroom at the same time as her and some other cheerleaders. She was telling them how she had given West a blow job in the guys' bathroom that morning. That particular image was one I wanted to cut out of my brain.

Even though being West's friend did not mean I had to

hang around him and his whatever she was, he had clearly been hurting earlier. His morning with his dad had to have been bad. Now it was time for the pep rally, though, so I wouldn't get a chance to talk to him about it.

I moved out of the way of traffic in the hallway as everyone hurried to the gym so I could text him back.

Okay. Do you want to talk after the pep rally?

I sent the message and waited a minute to see if he replied.

"No, I want to talk now." His voice was in my ear as his hand wrapped around my arm. Then he was moving me away from the crowd and down the empty hallway.

I didn't ask where we were going. I just went.

He opened the door to a classroom that didn't look like it was used anymore and guided me inside.

There were no desks in here. It was a small empty room with only one window. I turned to face him as the door clicked closed.

West closed the distance between us, but he didn't touch me. He just stared down at me as if he were searching for some answer.

"I can't do this tonight. I need to be home with my dad. He's just getting worse. What if I'm out playing a game and he . . . goes? What then, Maggie? How will I forgive myself for not being there beside him? For not

being there to hold my momma? She's gonna need me."
His eyes became watery even though I knew he wouldn't
cry, and he rubbed his hand over his mouth and nose.
"God, I can't do this. I can't. He loved football. We loved
it. But I love him more." He spoke each word as if it were
ripping him open.

I reached over and took both of his hands in mine. That
always seemed to calm him. "What would he want you to
do? If it were his choice, what would your dad want?" I
asked, already knowing the answer.

West sighed and hung his head. "He'd want me to play.
He always wanted me to play."

I didn't say anything more. I let him think about it as
we stood there. He laced his fingers through mine and held
on to me as if he needed me to survive.

"What about my momma? She'll be alone if I play."

"Is there someone you can ask to stay with her during
the game? Someone she trusts?" I asked him.

He lifted his head. "Your aunt."

Aunt Coralee would be there in a second if he'd
only ask. Brady would want her there. He wanted to
do something to help. If he thought his momma missing
his game to go sit with West's mother would help, he'd
want that.

"Ask her. She wants to help. Brady wants to help. Let

them. If anything were to happen, I'd have her text me immediately, and I'd be on that field to get you."

West's eyes had dried up and he nodded, his jaw clenched, as if he were fighting the urge to scream. I knew how that felt. I had actually screamed, though. I hadn't been able to control myself when I was faced with my mother's death.

"You're much stronger than you think," I told him.

He pulled me closer to him then bent his head and kissed the top of mine. It wasn't what I daydreamed about, but it was what I had. And I cherished it.

"Thank you," he said as his arms wrapped around me and held me against him. I wanted to sigh and sink into him, but that was not what this was. He was simply looking for comfort. And I would give him that.

"You're welcome," I replied against his chest.

We stood there for a few more moments before he stepped back and let his hands fall away from me. I felt cold without them. I wondered if he felt the same. Did I give him warmth the way he did me?

"I want you to meet my mom. She'd like you," he said as a small tired smile touched his lips. He was emotionally drained. This was exhausting him. I wondered if he slept at night.

"I'd like that. She sounds like an amazing woman."

He nodded. "She is."

The noise from the pep rally started up, and we heard the muted sounds of the school cheering.

"You'd better get in there," I said, hoping he wasn't in trouble for being late.

"I'm not going. I told Coach I had to go home and check on my dad. Boone told Coach about Dad this week. I didn't want him to know, but Boone was right that he needed to know. Now I can leave without having to explain myself and miss things like pep rallies without getting in trouble."

My uncle would be there when the time came, when West needed a father figure. I was thankful he had that. Uncle Boone was a good man. My mother had adored him. She'd talked about her big brother often. And they had the same eyes and the same smile. When Jorie had said she wanted me to go live with him, I'd hoped I would feel closer to my mother just by being near him. And I did.

"You want to go with me? Can you leave?" he asked me.

"Leave?" I wasn't sure I heard him right.

He nodded. "Yeah. Go home and meet my mom. Maybe if my dad's awake, you can meet him too. I mean if you're okay with seeing him. He looks . . . bad."

I would go see anyone this boy wanted me to.

"I'd like that."

His smile was the kind of smile that was so rare, you wanted to keep it. It made you sit around and think of things to do just to get that smile flashed at you. When his eyes were genuinely in it and he truly meant it, there was nothing that compared to West Ashby's smile.

CHAPTER 20

WEST

I pulled into my driveway and looked over at Maggie. She had agreed to come so easily. I wasn't sure I would have been brave enough to do that. We had walked out to my truck, and she'd texted her aunt to let her know she was leaving school with me and going to meet my parents.

I couldn't imagine bringing anyone else here right now. Not even Brady. Especially not Raleigh. This wasn't easy to see. But Maggie was sitting over there looking calm and strong. Always so strong.

"When I say my dad looks bad . . . he really does. He's so thin, his bones break easily now. And he's pale white. His skin almost seems translucent. It's tough to see. If you don't think you can handle it, I will understand."

Maggie turned to look at me, and her big green eyes were full of understanding. "I want to meet the man you adore. He's got to be special."

A jolt shot through my chest as I sat there and stared at her. Was she even real? How did she say the exact things I always needed to hear? I was beginning to think she was my guardian angel. If there were such a thing. God sure had let us down, but maybe he'd sent Maggie to me to give me the strength and comfort I was missing.

"Let's go on in, then. I texted Momma and told her we were coming." I hadn't told Momma about Maggie. We didn't talk much about anything except Dad. So when I texted her, I let her know Maggie was Brady's cousin and we'd become good friends.

Momma had said to bring her, that they would love to meet her. Dad was awake and talking some today. I hoped he'd be awake to see Maggie.

When we got to the front door, Maggie's fingers brushed my hand in that silent way of hers, reassuring me she was there and she wasn't leaving me. I loved it when she did that. She always seemed to know when I needed it most.

I opened the door and stepped back and motioned for Maggie to go inside. The entryway was empty, but I could smell cookies in the oven. Momma had gone and fixed us a snack. "Smells like Momma is in the kitchen," I told Maggie, then placed my hand on her lower back to lead her to meet my mother.

When we stepped inside the kitchen, Momma's back was turned, and she was getting down glasses for us. Her hair had been brushed and pulled into a ponytail, and she was wearing a nice shirt and jeans. She didn't spend much time getting fixed up anymore because she was afraid to leave Dad for too long. This was the most I'd seen her do to herself in a few weeks.

"Hey, Momma," I said quietly, not wanting to startle her.

She spun around, and her gaze went straight to Maggie. She was curious. I never brought girls here. Momma had only seen Raleigh a few times at my football games, and we'd been together a whole year.

"Hello, you must be Maggie," Momma said, walking over to greet us.

Maggie nodded. I had forgotten to tell my momma she didn't talk. My momma wasn't in on the town gossip, so she didn't know anything about Maggie's past. I opened my mouth to explain, when Maggie took a step toward her and held out her hand. "Yes, ma'am. It's nice to meet you."

I closed my mouth and stared at Maggie. I'd never heard her talk to anyone else. Not even her family. Yet she'd not hesitated to speak to my mother. One more thing about her that made her so incredibly special. After all she'd faced and all she'd been through, she still had compassion. She still sacrificed for others. I wasn't sure I could have done the same in her situation.

"It's a pleasure to meet you, too. Please call me Olivia. West doesn't bring friends home much anymore. I'm glad he felt like he could bring you," Momma said with a light in her eyes I hadn't seen in a while.

Maggie blushed and looked up at me.

"Maggie's special," I told Momma as I brushed my fingers over Maggie's hand the way she so often did mine.

"I can see that," Momma said, smiling. Her face was tired and weary, but my bringing Maggie here was making her happy. I realized Momma must feel so isolated with just us and no other life in the house. No distractions to help her cope with what we were facing.

"I think we both needed a friend who could understand us," Maggie said, surprising me yet again by speaking.

Mom turned her smile to me. She liked Maggie. But who wouldn't? "Your dad is awake. He needs to take his medicine soon. So you can bring her in there to meet him while he's not napping." Momma nodded toward the hallway.

He was in pain, was what that translated to. "If he needs

to go ahead and take his medicine now, I can introduce her to him another time."

She started shaking her head. "Oh no, he knows you're coming and bringing a friend already. I told him. He wants to meet her."

I glanced down at Maggie. "You ready?" I asked, wanting to give her one last chance to change her mind.

She nodded, and all the encouragement I needed was in her eyes.

I didn't care that my mother would see me; I needed to hold Maggie's hand right now. Slipping my hand over hers, I held it tightly. Then we walked down the hall to my parents' bedroom.

I eased the door open slowly and peeked inside.

"Stop being quiet, boy. I hear you. Come on in." He wheezed then coughed. It was a much weaker version of the booming voice I'd always known.

Maggie didn't pause but walked right inside with her hand still firmly tucked in mine.

"That's the prettiest friend you ever brought home," he said, smiling as if he weren't hurting all over.

"Thank you," Maggie said.

"I thought I raised you better," my dad said, still wheezing through his words. "Girl who looks like this one ain't for friendship. You're supposed to snatch her up."

Maggie laughed beside me, and Dad's grin grew.

"He's got a train of girls waiting for their turn. He doesn't need to add another to the long line," she replied, and my dad laughed. It wasn't the deep belly laugh he used to do, but it was the first laugh I'd heard from him in a while.

After he coughed and got his breath back, he looked at me. "Got a line, do you now?"

I shrugged. I didn't talk about girls with Dad much. Not after he caught me looking at porn on the computer when I was thirteen and gave me the sex talk. We talked football, school, life. But not girls.

"Yes. You should hear the girls in the stands at the pep rallies. He's very popular with them," Maggie informed Dad.

He laughed again. "I'm sure you got boys lining up for you, too. If this one is too blind to lay claim, I don't doubt one of them will."

My smile left. I didn't want to think about that. Maggie was meeting my momma and my dad. What if she started talking to another guy? What if she wasn't just mine anymore?

Dad let out another laugh, and I lifted my gaze to see him looking directly at me. "Ain't fun to think about, is it?" he said.

My gut twisted and felt sour. I didn't like thinking about that, and my dad clearly knew it.

"All this laughter in here. What in the world am I missing?" Momma asked as she stepped inside, looking happier than I'd seen her in a long time. Hearing Dad laugh was good for both of us.

"There's my favorite girl," Dad said as Momma walked over to him. He still looked at her like she was his every wish come true. Momma bent down and kissed his lips. "I had to go make these two a snack. Tonight is game night, and West needs some carbs."

Dad looked from Momma to me. "You gonna win tonight?" he asked. This was always our thing.

"You know it," I replied just like I always did.

"That's my boy."

It Takes Years Before They Wise Up
CHAPTER 21

MAGGIE

I had texted with Aunt Coralee several times during the game to check on Mr. Ashby, or Jude, as he'd told me to call him. She had assured me he was sleeping and everything was fine. I wanted to be able to reassure West that everything was okay every time he looked up in the stands at me.

He did it several times, and each time I nodded.

Through it all, he managed to run in a touchdown and make several plays I didn't understand but that, according to Uncle Boone, who explained things as they happened, were very impressive. West was always there for Brady to make the best plays.

I knew tonight he wouldn't be going to the field party. He was worried about being away from his dad. I had asked Aunt Coralee if I could go home after the game instead of going to the field party with Brady. Even though I was glad I'd met his parents, emotionally, I was spent.

Although Jude had talked to me, it had been hard for him, and he was using all the energy he had to talk to us. He gasped for breath and coughed. Then watching the way he stared at his wife like he adored her had broken my heart.

I couldn't remember a time in my life when my parents had looked at each other that way. I could remember them fighting and yelling, and they'd always made up. Yet not once did they look at each other the way West's parents did.

To think that they would lose that was so incredibly sad.

As the crowd made their way out to their cars, I followed Uncle Boone as he went to wait on Brady to come out of the locker room. I wanted to see West before I left. Leaving his dad today had been hard on him. He'd held on to my hand the entire ride back to my house. If I could've held his hand on to the football field, I would have.

"There's West," Uncle Boone said, nodding toward the field house. "I reckon you'll want to go see him. I think he's probably looking for you."

I glanced up at Uncle Boone, and he gave me an understanding smile. I hoped he didn't think what West and I were doing was anything more than friendship. I had explained it to Aunt Coralee because she'd asked me. But I hadn't really explained it to Uncle Boone.

I nodded and headed over to West. But Serena got to him before I could. She squealed and wrapped her arms around him. I stopped and waited. I had come to realize that sometimes West needed me, but other times he needed her. Or someone like her. I wasn't sure if this was one of those times.

West listened to her talk, and he gave her a nod. I decided it was Serena time not Maggie time, and I turned and headed back to Uncle Boone. He was standing where I'd left him, watching me. He didn't look happy, but he didn't look mad, either. Just concerned.

I stopped when I got back to his side, and we waited on Brady.

After a few moments Uncle Boone cleared his throat. "Boys don't always make the right decisions. It takes years before they become men and wise up."

He didn't have to explain. I was already starting to understand.

"You deserve more, Maggie. He's hurting, but you've had your share of hurt too, sweetheart."

I knew Uncle Boone meant well. And I also knew he was right. I did deserve more, and I knew it wouldn't be from West. He never promised me more than friendship, and friendship was what he needed from me. And until he didn't need me anymore, I'd be there for him. Even if it was hard, and even if I had flutters from time to time. It was my job to remember he had no other deeper feelings for me. I would guard myself. I had made it through hell and survived. I could do this.

"We killed it!" Brady's voice boomed, and I looked out to see him walking toward us, beaming at his dad. Uncle Boone stood there with pride etched on his face. I imagined this was why it was so hard for West. This was one of the things he'd already lost.

"Good game, son." Uncle Boone patted Brady on the back. "You headed to the field?"

"Yeah, you coming, Maggie?" he asked, looking at me.

I shook my head.

He looked relieved and concerned at the same time.

"She's gonna go on home with me tonight," Uncle Boone told him, not mentioning my visit to West's this afternoon.

"All right, I won't be home too late," he assured his dad, then turned and headed toward Ivy, who was waiting for him.

I glanced back in West's direction, and our eyes collided. He was already headed my way. Serena was following behind him. This was not something I wanted to do in front of Uncle Boone.

"You want to wait on him to get here, or you want to go?" Uncle Boone asked.

I glanced up at Uncle Boone and gave him an apologetic smile. I knew he didn't agree with this situation, and I loved that he cared enough about me to be worried. But I wasn't running off on West. Not after seeing Brady with his dad and recognizing West wouldn't ever have that again.

"Hey," West said, bringing my attention back to him.

Serena stopped behind him. The look on her face was pure annoyance.

I moved my gaze away from her and back to West. I smiled at him. I wanted him to know everything was good. I'd text him later and tell him "good game."

"You going to the field?"

I shook my head.

"She's not going. So can we leave now?" Serena asked, reaching out and taking West's arm.

He didn't pull away from her, and I refused to let that hurt me.

"You going home?" he asked me.

I nodded.

"You played a good game," Uncle Boone said, placing

his hand on my shoulder. "That touchdown was impressive. Your dad will be happy to hear about it." Then he started steering me toward the parking lot. "Y'all have a good night now. Maggie and I are headed home."

He hadn't left any room for argument.

West looked torn. Like he wanted to stop me, but he didn't know what to do. I couldn't make that decision for him. I lifted my hand and gave him a small wave before turning and walking away with Uncle Boone.

She Will Always Be Just My Friend

CHAPTER 22

WEST

I didn't leave the house all weekend except to run to the store for some milk and eggs. Once Maggie had left with her uncle on Friday, I'd gotten it through Serena's head that I was going home. Alone.

When I got home, Dad had been asleep, but I'd sat and talked to Momma about the game and Maggie. She really liked Maggie. She also wanted to know why Coralee thought that Maggie didn't talk. Momma had been smart enough to know something was up and didn't tell Coralee that Maggie had in fact talked when she was here.

It was the first thing she'd asked me when I'd gotten home. I knew she was reading more into things with Maggie than was true. She might have wanted us to be together, but I wasn't in the right mindset to have a relationship with someone like Maggie. Someone who deserved so much more than I had to give.

Explaining that to Momma wasn't really a good idea, though. She'd worry about me. And she already had enough to worry about. We both did.

Saturday I'd spent the day in Dad's room watching college football. When he was awake, we talked some about the game Friday night. Mostly I talked and he listened. It was hard for him to talk now. Breathing was getting harder and harder on him. The hospice worker came, and I stayed with Dad while I could. I only stepped out when she and Momma bathed him.

Sunday was a repeat of Saturday, except we watched the NFL games. Momma curled up on the bed with us, and we talked. We talked about our first camping trip and how Momma had screamed when the black bear had gotten into our cooler. Then we laughed about the first time we had taken Momma fishing. She'd been horrified by the fact we put live crickets on the hook.

Dad also wanted to know about Maggie. She'd charmed him easily enough. He had warned me not to mess that up, saying she was a keeper. Momma had patted my hand as if to agree with him.

Each night after Dad went to sleep, I'd go to my room and text Maggie. She always answered, and eventually we'd end up talking on the phone until we both fell asleep.

By Monday I was more than ready to see her. Dad had actually slept through the night and seemed better this morning. Momma had been happy about that, and leaving them hadn't been as hard.

My good morning was over right quick, though, when I saw Serena talking to Maggie at her locker. I could tell by the look on Serena's face that they weren't having a nice chat. Maggie had backed away from her and was pushed up against the locker door, her green eyes wide and nervous. That didn't make me fucking happy at all.

I shoved through the crowd, and eventually everyone moved for me. When I got close enough, I heard Serena: "He fucks me. He doesn't want you. Back off."

"Get the hell away from Maggie. Now," I roared as I moved in between them and put my hands on Serena's shoulders to move her back. "Don't ever. Ever. Get in her face again. Don't breathe the same air she breathes. Don't even fucking look at her. Do you understand what I'm saying?"

Serena's eyes went wide with surprise. She hadn't expected me to catch her. She'd been furious that I'd wanted to go see Maggie after the game. Until then she hadn't seen her as competition.

"She's flirting with you. She thinks she can have you. I was just telling her what we've been doing. That you just see her as a friend," Serena began explaining as if she were completely innocent.

I felt Maggie's body move behind me, and I reached back to touch her hand. She wasn't leaving. I missed her. Serena wasn't gonna mess up my morning with her misplaced jealousy.

"You don't know what she can have. But I'll tell you what you can't have. Me. We had a fun little fling, but that's done. We're done." I didn't leave room for her to reply. I turned my back on her, knowing we had the entire hallway's attention now. I knew she wouldn't stand there, begging me to look at her. She had more pride than that. So I wasn't surprised when she stalked away. And then everyone went back to their business.

Maggie's eyes were still wide and so damn pretty as she stared up at me.

"I'm sorry about that. It's my fault. I make stupid-ass decisions, and they should never affect you."

She moved her hand to squeeze mine. "It's okay," she whispered so softly, no one would hear her.

"It's not okay. No one talks to you like that. No one," I said, feeling my anger start to build again. I hated seeing Maggie afraid.

She gave me a small smile then slipped her hand from mine and reached for her book bag on the floor. I watched her as she got her books, wishing I had her alone so we could talk. So I could hear her voice. I had heard it over the phone just last night, but it was always different in person.

Stepping close to her, I inhaled and let her vanilla scent wash over me. I could take that with me to first period. Since I couldn't take her.

When she turned around, we were so close, our bodies almost touched.

Almost immediately a hand landed on my shoulder and squeezed hard. "Friends. Remember?" Brady's voice wasn't threatening, but it sure wasn't friendly, either.

I took one more deep inhale then stepped back. Maggie glanced at Brady, then smiled one last time at me. Her cheeks turned pink as she held her books close to her chest and hurried away.

Once she was out of sight, I turned to Brady. He was frowning. "That wasn't friendly. That was 'I'm about to eat you up in this hallway in front of everyone.' That's what that was. I saw it. So did everyone else. And did she . . . did I see her mouth move?"

She wouldn't want him to know. It wasn't something she was ready to share. I shook my head. "No. We just communicate differently. That's all that was."

Brady cocked an eyebrow. He knew I was full of shit. I had wanted to be as close to her as I could get. "Remember, she's fragile. Don't break her."

He didn't know how wrong he was. Maggie was one of the strongest people I knew.

"I told you already, I would never hurt her. I was making sure she was okay. Serena was being nasty, and I fixed that. I won't let someone hurt her. Trust me."

Brady shook his head, his frown still in place. "I'm trying to. But I see the way you look at her."

"Just because I want something, doesn't mean I'm cruel enough to take it. I'd never do that to her. She is just my friend. She will always be just my friend."

No One Else Is Fun to Talk To
CHAPTER 23

MAGGIE

The rest of the week things with West's dad seemed better. He was still having problems breathing, but he was awake more. In pain less, or so it seemed. He didn't need to take as much of the medicine that kept him drugged up. I'd gone to visit him on Wednesday evening. West had come to get me after his football practice, and we had eaten dinner with his mother. Then we went to talk with his dad.

On Thursday, West met me at the door of the cafeteria and insisted I eat at his table. Since Serena was no longer there, I agreed. The guys were still trying to figure out our friendship. It didn't make sense to them, but by Friday they had accepted that I was going to be sitting with them from now on, and they all seemed okay with that.

West and I were . . . well, I didn't know what we were. We texted all throughout the day and talked on the phone every evening. We didn't just talk about his dad or my past; we talked about life. He told me stories about him and Brady as kids, and I told him about my years as a cheer-leader in junior high.

But I found our situation increasingly confusing. Like when West would get close to me and breathe deeply like he was taking me in. Or the times he held his hand on my back longer than necessary. Or the time Nash sat down beside me and started flirting, and West had gotten angry. He tried not to show it, but everyone saw it, including Brady.

Even though he did all those things, he still flirted with the girls at school who came on to him. Although he wasn't having sex with any of them in the restroom or getting attached to any of them, he also never mentioned our kiss or acted as if he'd like to try it again.

He hadn't mentioned what his plans were after the foot-ball game Friday night nor had he asked me about mine. So I asked Aunt Coralee if I could please go straight home and go to bed. I was tired. She agreed, and I left right after the game with her while Uncle Boone stayed to talk to Brady.

West had scored three touchdowns, and the smile on

his face had made everything that was wrong, right. I loved seeing him happy. I wished I could be there when he told his dad all about it.

I let the week's events replay in my mind while I showered and got ready for bed. Brady seemed less annoyed with me lately, and I knew it was because he didn't have to take me everywhere anymore. His parents had stopped trying to foist me off on him constantly. Dinnertime was easier, and I liked listening to all of them talk.

I also let the idea of starting to talk in public again roll around in my head. I had talked to West's parents but only because I hadn't wanted to make things difficult for them with my silence. And, if I never got a chance to speak to his dad again, I didn't want to regret staying silent.

I wanted to be a part of this family, but as long as I didn't talk or share my day-to-day life, I remained an outsider. If I started talking to my aunt and uncle, eventually they were going to want me to talk about what I'd seen. About what had happened. I didn't want to. I was no longer terrified to hear my own voice—talking to West had shown me I could hear myself again and not fall apart—but I wasn't ready to talk about my mother . . . or my father. The Higgenses knew all there was to know. If I could trust them not to force me to talk about that night, then I could talk to them.

I finished showering then stepped out and towel dried

my hair before slipping the towel around my body and hurrying back to my room.

Stepping through the bedroom door, I started to scream when I saw West standing inside. I quickly slapped one hand over my mouth while gripping the towel tightly around me with the other.

"West?" I asked, adjusting so I could hold my towel around me with both hands.

His eyes weren't on my face but on my very bare legs. I was tempted to run back into the hallway.

"West?" I repeated.

His eyes snapped up to meet mine, and he grinned sheepishly. "Sorry. Didn't mean to scare you. I texted you that I was coming up, but you didn't answer."

"Coming up?" I repeated, still very confused.

He nodded to the window. "This was Brady's room most of my life. I've been climbing in that window since I was seven."

Oh. But why was he here?

"You left . . . the game . . . and you didn't go to the field party. I waited for you."

This. This was what confused me. I didn't understand when he did things like this. He hadn't asked me all day about my plans tonight. I assumed he had some of his own. I hadn't known he wanted to see me.

"I left with Aunt Coralee. You didn't mention seeing me afterward."

Now he was the one who looked confused. Why was he confused? He was the one giving me crazy mixed signals! "I figured you knew I'd want to see you. Hang out."

I shook my head. I didn't know anything.

He grinned at me this time. "Well, always assume we have plans. You're the only friend I want to hang out with. Now, could you maybe get some clothes on? That's uh . . . distracting."

"You do know you came into my room uninvited, right? If I had known you were coming, I'd have been dressed."

He smirked. "I texted you."

"I was in the shower."

"Minor detail."

This time I laughed. But I quickly caught myself and bit my lip, hoping Aunt Coralee didn't hear me. "Turn around," I whispered.

"Why?"

"So I can get my clothes on."

"Okay, yeah, that," he said, and turned to face the wall.

I went over and grabbed a pair of panties from my drawer and then some leggings and a baggy T-shirt. I had never dressed with a guy in the same room. Even though he wasn't looking, it still made me nervous. I dressed quickly and reached up to run my fingers through my wet hair. Crap. I'd forgotten about my hair.

"I'm done," I told him as I turned to search for my brush.

"Nice," he said, which made me pause and look over my shoulder at him.

He winked. I hated it when he winked at me. Mostly because I loved it when he winked. I hated that I loved it. Because friends did not get birds in their tummies over winks.

"You should wear leggings more often," he said, and I set my attention on looking for a brush. When I finally found it, I started pulling it through my tangled hair before turning back to him.

"How was the field party?" I asked, sitting down on the end of my bed.

He shrugged and sat down beside me. "Boring. You weren't there. No one else is fun to talk to."

I rolled my eyes, making him chuckle.

"Your aunt and uncle check on you at night?"

I shook my head. I locked my door at night. I have nightmares and, although I didn't scream in them, I often cried and whimpered, saying things I didn't want them to hear.

"Can I stay a while if we whisper?"

Like I would tell him no. I never told him no. Even though I should tell him no. . . . It wouldn't hurt him for me to tell him no, and he could stand to hear it more often.

"Of course."

You're Insane If You Think
I'd Make a Move on My Cousin

CHAPTER 24

WEST

She'd fallen asleep on me—literally, on me—about an hour ago. But I was still here. Her head had been on my shoulder when she'd nodded off and had gradually moved its way to my chest. I had to get out of here before Brady got home and saw my truck parked down the street. His parents might not notice it, but he would. He would also know I was in her room and how I got there. I wasn't going to push my luck with him.

Easing out from under her, I pulled the covers up so she wouldn't get cold. Just as I was about to move away, she began to whimper. It was soft, but it was a cry. Then she began to kick and shake her head as the whimpering got louder.

I have nightmares every night. I see my mother die over

and over again. Her words replayed in my head. Was that what this was? I began to rub my hand up and down her arm as I assured her she was okay and I was here.

It didn't help. She kept kicking and then started to moan pitifully.

I hated seeing her like this. Lost in a horror she couldn't escape. It wasn't a nightmare. Those weren't real. Those you could wake up from. This was a memory that haunted her. One she'd never wake up from.

I crawled in bed and lay behind her, wrapping my arms around her and pulling her against my chest. I kept whispering in her ear that I was here. That she was in my arms and I wasn't leaving her. That she'd be okay.

Slowly, she began to ease. She quit kicking and her terrified sounds stopped. Then her fingers wrapped firmly around my arm. She wasn't letting me go. Even in her sleep she knew I was here, and she was keeping me close.

That felt good. For once, I had helped her. She'd been my rock and my source of peace, but I was never one for her. I thought she'd gone and lived her hell alone. But in reality, she was still living it, and I could do for her what she did for me. Hold on to her so she never lost herself.

Someone was jerking my body back and forth. Groggily, I opened my eyes to see why. It was still dark out. I blinked and looked down to see that Maggie had turned and was now facing me, tucked in close to my body.

A hand on my arm tightened. Apparently, I hadn't woken up on my own. I looked up to see Brady scowling at me.

"What. The. Fuck," he growled. "I trusted you." He was keeping his voice down, which was good. Brady I could handle, but Boone would kill me.

"She had a nightmare. I was just helping her, and then I fell asleep too. I swear to God, that was it."

Brady's scowl didn't lift. "Why were you in her room? It's after midnight. I know you, West, and you don't crawl in bed with girls and do nothing."

He was right about that. Except with Maggie. I did crawl in bed and do nothing with Maggie.

"I would never touch her, Brady. I swear it. She's my friend, and she needed me. I'm not trying to do anything more with her."

Brady finally looked like he might believe me. "She's dressed," he said.

"Yeah, and so am I. My boots are even still on," I pointed out.

Brady backed up and nodded for me to move.

I eased away from Maggie and covered her up. Brady was her cousin, but I didn't like the idea of him seeing her in those skintight leggings. Her shirt was bunched around her waist, and you could see a little slice of skin on her stomach. I didn't want him seeing that either.

"Don't come back in her room at night."

I wasn't going to argue with him, but he was stupid if he thought I wouldn't come back. If she wanted me here, I'd be back every damn night to check on her.

"We talked. She fell asleep, then she started having a nightmare about the same time I was leaving. I calmed her down and fell asleep in the process."

Brady gave me a hard nod. "Fine. Now leave."

I would go, but he was leaving too. "I will. But so are you."

He looked at me like I had lost my mind. "What?"

I looked back at Maggie sleeping curled up alone in the bed. "If I leave, so do you. She locks her door at night. How'd you get in?" I asked him.

"I know how to get into my old room when it's locked. Besides, once I saw your truck parked down the road, I knew where you were and how you got in here."

I trusted Brady, but I didn't like that. "I leave, you leave," I repeated.

"Are you serious?" he asked.

"Very."

Brady shook his head and opened the bedroom door. "I

swear to God, West. You're insane if you think I'd make a move on my cousin."

I didn't think he would. I just didn't like him being in her room while she was asleep. She hadn't invited him in. It was an invasion of her privacy.

When I'd finally gotten home and into my own bed, I'd gone to sleep hoping I'd wake up to a repeat of last weekend with my dad. I didn't get it.

Instead I was woken by the sounds of an ambulance outside the house, and my mother's frantic voice. My heart slammed against my chest, and I moved fast. I ran from my room toward the front of the house where I heard Momma.

"He's down the hall!" she shouted at the paramedics who were already rushing through the door. "Hurry! He's throwing up so much blood. Hurry! Please!" Momma was crying pitifully, and the paramedics moved fast. I backed up and let them pass, then went to my mother, who was holding on to the front door as if she were about to collapse. She had blood all over her clothing. And tears were running down her face. "We're gonna lose him. Oh God, West, we're gonna lose him." She sobbed as her knees buckled.

I hurried over to her and held her against my chest. "He needs us to be strong right now. We can break down later.

But we need to show him that we can handle this. If he sees you cracking, it will be even harder on him." As I urged her to do what I wasn't sure I could do myself, I felt like Maggie was right there with me saying those words in my ear. Reminding me this wasn't about me right now. That I was strong enough for this.

Momma nodded and wiped at her face. "You're right. He needs us to be strong," she repeated. "Help me remember that." She patted my arms I'd wrapped around her. "I need to change and go with them to the hospital."

"I'll drive you. Go get changed, and we'll follow. They aren't going to let you in the back. They'll need all the room to help Dad."

She nodded again, but I could tell she didn't like the idea of his leaving this house without her.

I held her as they brought out my father, unconscious and covered in blood. Seeing him like that brought on a new, deeper sorrow. One I hadn't experienced yet.

"We're coming, honey. We're right behind you. Be strong for us. We'll be waiting on you," Momma called after him.

"Go on and get cleaned up," I told her.

She held on to my arms for a few more seconds as they put him in the back of the ambulance. Then she hurried down the hall to change.

I jumped in the shower and cleaned off before throwing on some jeans and a T-shirt. Once we got to the hospital, I'd find a cleaning service to call about coming to clean up their room. I wanted it nice and ready when Dad came back home. I also didn't want Momma cleaning it up.

When I stepped out of my own room, Momma stepped out into the hall from hers. We looked at each other for a moment. "He needs us to be strong for him," I reminded her. I wanted her to find her inner strength too. In case this was it. If we had to say good-bye to him soon, I wanted her to be ready to give him that without breaking down.

I just hoped to God I could do it. Momma nodded once more and headed for the door. I followed behind her as I texted Maggie. I was going to need her now more than ever.

I Need You Here

CHAPTER 25

MAGGIE

They took him to the hospital in an ambulance. I need you.

I kept reading West's text over and over as Aunt Coralee, Uncle Boone, Brady, and I drove to the hospital.

He hadn't given me details. He just said he needed me. I had jumped out of bed and gotten dressed without thinking of how I was going to get to the hospital. When I hurried into the hallway to go to the bathroom so I could brush my teeth, Uncle Boone had been walking up the stairs with the morning paper. I'd handed him my phone so he could see the text message. He read it, then went to wake up Aunt Coralee and Brady.

No one was talking. Brady kept bouncing his knee nervously as he stared out the window. He'd been the first one in the living room after his dad had woken them all up. The panic written across his face was what only a real friend would feel.

I wasn't sure I'd had that, not from any of my friends. I was thankful West did.

"I need to tell the guys," Brady finally said. "It's time they knew. They'll want to be there with him too."

Uncle Boone nodded. "I agree. After we get there and you've seen them, you can go find a quiet place and call. But not the whole team. Just the ones he's close to. He needs his real friends around him right now."

I wasn't sure West would want that, but if this was the end, then he needed it.

"Did he text you?" Brady asked me.

I nodded.

"Did he give you any details?"

I shook my head and handed him my phone.

He read the text several times before handing back the phone to me.

"Thank you," he said. "For being there for him. I don't understand whatever it is y'all have, but thank you."

He didn't have to thank me. It was West. I'd do anything for him.

My phone dinged, and we all tensed up. I wanted to hurry and get to him.

He has a tumor pressing against a vein or something. They have him back there. That's all I know. We're on the fourth floor left wing waiting room.

I quickly typed: We are on our way. Almost there.

Then I handed the phone to Brady. He read the text to his parents. Then the phone dinged again, and he read the incoming text silently before handing it to me:

Good. I need you here.

I closed my eyes tightly and prayed. I wasn't sure what to pray for because I knew West's dad couldn't be saved from this. But I prayed anyway.

Once we arrived at the hospital, Uncle Boone let us out at the entrance before he went to park. I didn't wait on anyone. I ran inside and headed for the elevators. If West got the news his dad had passed away, I wanted to be there beside him. I wanted him to have what I hadn't. Someone who understood.

When the elevator door opened, I hurried on and pressed the button. When the doors opened again on the fourth floor, there stood West. His eyes were bloodshot, and they locked on mine. He'd been waiting on me.

"Hey," he said in a hoarse whisper.

I stepped out of the elevator and reached out my hand to take his. "Hey."

"They just let Mom go back," he said, tightening his hold on my hand and pulling me closer to him. "Said he was stable, but there isn't much they can do other than try to make him comfortable."

For months he'd feared going to sleep and waking up to find his dad gone. Today was a close call. I threaded my fingers through his. "Let's go back to the waiting room. They'll come get you soon."

"Yeah," he agreed.

The white walls were so sterile. Hospitals had always felt cold to me. I wouldn't want to die here. I'd like to die somewhere I loved, somewhere that made me feel safe. Which, finally, made me realize what I would pray for. I closed my eyes and said a silent prayer that Jude Ashby didn't have to die here. That he could die at home. A place he loved.

"Who brought you?" West asked as I opened my eyes.

"Uncle Boone, Aunt Coralee, and Brady. They're right behind me. I just ran when we got out of the car. I didn't want you to be here . . . without me."

West's hand squeezed mine, then he brushed his thumb against my thumb. "Thank you."

I remembered his text about needing me. He needed me for his own reasons. Ones I understood. But I needed him, too. Because in three short weeks he'd wedged his way into my heart.

I'd realized this morning, after seeing that text and not being there with him, that nothing was as important as getting to this hospital. I had never been in love, so I had nothing to compare it to, but there was no question in my mind that West Ashby had become the most important person in my life. I was in love with him. I could be whatever it was he needed me to be. Even if that would always be just a friend.

CHAPTER 26

WEST

I had expected Maggie to move her hand away from mine when her family showed up. But she hadn't. Not even when her aunt and uncle had both looked directly at our joined hands. She had stayed close beside me, holding on to me while they'd all talked. Coralee had kissed the top of my head and told me she loved me.

Boone had nodded and patted my shoulder. Then Brady had taken the seat on my other side, silently letting me know he was there for me. Having people here was a relief. Especially for Momma. I didn't want her to think we were alone.

I had Maggie, that was all I needed, but the Higgenses being here made it easier for Momma.

"I'll be back in a few minutes," Brady said as he stood up and walked down the hallway.

"He's going to tell the other guys. They ones you're close to," Maggie whispered, barely moving her lips. Her aunt and uncle were talking over by the coffee machine. They weren't looking at us.

"He tell you that?" I asked

"Yes, he told all of us in the car. He's worried about you."

It was time they knew. I should have told them sooner. But I'd had Maggie, and telling anyone else wasn't something I cared about doing.

"He's going. I can feel it," I said it out loud, needing to hear myself admit it.

"You'll hurt. It's the worst pain. But you're strong, and you'll make it through. You'll have his memory. That won't ever leave you." She stopped talking when her aunt turned around. I was sure she hadn't heard Maggie's quiet whisper.

I held on to her words. She knew what this felt like. She was being honest with me. She wasn't patting my arm and telling me that I'd be okay or that she was sorry for me. I'd be getting a lot of that soon.

"This morning my momma—God, you should have seen her lose it. That was tough." My mother sobbing as she held on to the door was an image that would never leave my mind. I'd always remember that horrible moment.

Maggie turned her head and pressed her face to my arm. "But she has you. You have each other. Hold on to that," she said with her mouth hidden from her family.

I pressed a kiss to the top of her head. I didn't care if they saw me. I wanted her to know she was important. That I cherished her. I would always cherish her and our friendship.

Brady came back into the room and sat down next to me. "I called the guys. They're on their way here. They want to be here with you and, whether you want to admit it or not, you need them too."

He was wrong. I didn't need them. I had who I needed tucked close to my side. But I didn't tell him that. I just nodded. He wouldn't understand.

Two hours later the guys were all filling up the waiting room. So was the entire football coaching staff. Ryker's and Nash's parents had both come. Asa's dad and Gunner's dad had also come.

No matter who came in, Maggie stayed by my side with her hand in mine. I knew she wouldn't let go. That bit of comfort helped.

The guys didn't ask me why I hadn't told them. I figured Brady had made sure of that. They all came in and stood close, giving me their silent support.

A couple of the parents said how sorry they were to hear about my dad. That if we needed anything, to please call them. They'd bring over meals and that kind of thing. I nodded and tensed up each time one of them mentioned how hard this must be on me.

Momma finally appeared from her visit with Dad, and her eyes widened at the waiting room full of people. Then she searched for me. I stood up and took Maggie with me. She didn't question it, just went with me, her hand still in mine.

When I reached Momma, she gave me a teary smile that didn't touch her eyes. "He's okay right now, but he's not awake yet. If you want to go back and sit with him a while, you can. It's only two at a time, though, for a few more hours."

I had to go see my dad. Maggie's hand eased from mine, and she looked up at me. I could see the encouragement there. She wanted me to go with my momma. In case this was it, we both needed to be at his side.

"I'm here," she said softly. "Go."

I nodded then followed my mother down the hall. She stopped outside my dad's door, and I could see him hooked up to machines, looking too frail in that hospital bed. The last time he'd been in one of those, he'd been bigger. Not so sick. Things had changed so much over the past couple of months.

"Talk to him. I think he can hear us. In case . . . in case

this is it. Tell him everything you want him to know," she said, the words catching in her throat as her eyes welled with tears.

I went inside first and made my way over to the side of the bed. His breathing was weak and raspy like he was struggling for each breath. Last weekend he'd been laughing with us. I knew we'd never get a weekend like that again. It had been our last.

"Hey, Dad," I said as I stood there staring down at him. Memorizing this moment. I needed all my memories to keep with me. "I know you're not a fan of this place, but you should see the crowd you have in the waiting room. They're packing the joint," I said, glancing over at my mother on the other side of the bed as she slipped her hand under my dad's.

"Maggie's out there too. She was here almost as soon as we arrived. If they'd let more people back, I know she'd want to come see you."

I wasn't convinced he could hear me even though Momma thought so. All we could do was hope he could. There was so much I wanted to say, but how was I supposed to say it?

Maggie hadn't gotten a chance to say anything to her mother. I wouldn't not take my chance.

"I love you. I'm proud to be your son." I choked up

as the words came out. "My whole life you've been our rock. You've been the strong shoulders we leaned on. A kid couldn't have asked for a better father. I have the best d—" I stopped and swallowed hard as I watched his chest rise with each labored breath. "I have the best dad. But I want you to know, I can be the man now. I can take care of Momma, and I swear to you I will. She won't ever be alone. I'll make sure of that. I'll make you proud of me. Don't worry about us. We will miss you every day. Your memory will always be with us. But I won't let you down. I'll be the man you raised me to be."

Momma let out a sob that sent the tears pooling in my eyes down my face. I loved this man so much. Life without him wasn't something I'd ever imagined. Facing it now seemed impossible. Even as I promised him I would be the rock Momma needed.

I Won't Have Regrets

CHAPTER 27

MAGGIE

After West went back to see his dad, I took a seat beside Aunt Coralee. She patted my leg and told me she was proud of me for being there for West. She didn't add that I had my own share of pain when it came to losing a parent, but the way she spoke, I could tell she was thinking it.

Brady was over with Asa, Gunner, Ryker, and Nash, all talking quietly. As if they knew death was near and they weren't sure how to handle it. When you hadn't dealt with death, you didn't understand. That had been me once. Before.

Over the next hour, Raleigh arrived, along with other people I recognized from school. I wasn't sure Raleigh being here was a good thing. She glanced over at me when she first arrived, and the hatred on her face was obvious. Just like Serena, she was confused about what I actually was to West. They had both had him in ways I never would. But then, I knew a part of West that they never would. I understood the difference. They didn't.

Uncle Boone stood with the coaches as they talked and drank coffee. Deep concern was written across all their faces. West was loved. And from the way the others spoke of his dad, so was Jude.

The hours passed, and we all waited. Every hour West was back there meant another hour he'd had with his dad. I hoped he said everything he wanted to say. That when his dad took his last breath, West had no regrets.

I watched as Raleigh walked over to talk to Brady. He was polite to her, but I could see he wasn't thrilled she was here.

Suddenly Aunt Coralee spoke beside me. "We were there with you the day it happened. You probably don't remember. You weren't handling it well. Bless your heart, how could you? My heart broke as I watched you pull away from everyone. But you're with us now, and we love you, Maggie. I want you to know that. I know you don't want to talk about it, but sitting here, watching this, I want you to know we were there. Jorie was there. We made sure no one got near you or pushed you to do anything you didn't want to do."

I did remember them being there. I had been lost in my own grief, but I remembered seeing my aunt's tear-streaked face as she'd kept guard over me. I hadn't forgotten that. I hadn't cared at the time, but looking back I'm glad she'd done it.

I looked over at her and smiled. I wanted to tell her that I knew. That I was thankful they'd been there. But my emotions were too raw today. Knowing what West was going through was enough. I couldn't also try to speak to her for the first time.

The day rolled away as the night came. The waiting room remained full. Brady had dozed off in his chair and Nash had lain down on several chairs to take a nap.

Raleigh had left, thankfully. I'd breathed a sigh of relief when she'd given up on waiting for West.

It was close to eight in the evening when West walked through the doors. His eyes scanned the waiting room until they found me. I stood up, my stomach in knots. As much as I had prepared myself for this, I wasn't sure I could be strong.

West held out his hand for me, and I walked over and took it. "He can have more visitors now. I'd like that to be you," he said close to my ear.

I squeezed his hand. He looked up from me to the others waiting.

"He's . . . stable. Struggling . . . to breathe. But he's sleeping," West said to everyone. "Thank y'all for coming. For being here. Knowing we have people out here who care means a lot. Especially to my mom. So thanks for that."

West moved his attention back to me. "You ready?"

I nodded.

His fingers threaded with mine, and we walked back through those doors I'd been watching all day.

His dad's room had large windows so the nurses could watch him from their station. From the hallway I could see his mother's head resting on the bed beside his dad's arm. Her hand was locked tightly with his. She was holding on to him, as if she could keep him here that way.

"I think Momma's asleep. She's cried a lot today. It's been draining," he said as he opened the door and stood back for me to go in. His hand touched my lower back and led me over to the sofa against the wall.

He sat down and put his arm along the back of the sofa. "Come here. Sit with me."

It was obvious he wanted me close, and I understood. I sat down, and he pulled me closer to him, his arm around my shoulders. I rested my head on his chest and watched his father's uneven breathing. Each gasp seemed like it was a fight for him.

"I won't have regrets," West said, then pressed a kiss to

the top of my head. "Thank you for that. For keeping my head on straight. If you hadn't helped me, I don't know if I'd have been able to do it today. But I did. I said everything to him I wanted him to know."

I tilted my head back so I could see his face. Each beautiful angle had become precious to me. I wanted to reach up and touch him. Reassure him. But that wasn't what we were.

He gazed down at me. There were no more words. My look was a silent reassurance I wasn't leaving and he had me.

Movement broke the spell, and we both turned to see that Olivia had raised her head and was looking at Jude, panicked. There was obvious relief on her face as she saw his chest rise and fall.

She touched his arm and let out a sigh. "I didn't mean to fall asleep," she said, sounding apologetic.

"You're exhausted, Momma. Dad would want you to rest," West told her.

Olivia turned her head to see us on the sofa. A tired smile touched her lips. "Hello, Maggie. I'm glad they've let you come back. If Jude were awake, he'd be all smiles and happy to see you with West."

I remembered the last time I'd see him. He'd been awake and laughing. Life could be so cruel.

"Can I get you anything?" I asked her. I wondered if she'd eaten at all.

She shook her head. "I'm fine, but thank you."

I watched her as she tucked his covers in around him and fussed over his pillow. West pulled me close to him again, and we sat there silently. Watching Jude breathe. There was nothing to say. In the face of sorrow and loss, no words could ever be adequate.

They Hadn't Left

CHAPTER 28

WEST

I had sent Maggie home with the Higgenses at ten. She hadn't wanted to leave me, but she'd needed to sleep. Momma and I would sleep in here. Boone promised to bring Maggie back first thing in the morning. She'd been my rock today. Letting her go hadn't been easy for me, but I could see the exhaustion in her eyes.

At 4:53 that morning my dad took his last breath. I hadn't been sleeping. I couldn't. Momma had, though, and I'd woken her before the nurses could arrive. She had kissed his face and told him over and over that she loved him, then curled into my arms and sobbed.

While I stood there holding her and watching as the nurses began undoing all the machines, I said my own silent good-bye. To the best man I would ever know. He had fought hard, but in the end I knew he couldn't hold on any longer. I'd promised him I'd take care of Momma, and I wouldn't let him down.

When it was time for us to leave, I held my mother in my arms, and we walked out that door for the last time. We made our way down the hall toward the waiting room door. I opened it, expecting it to be empty.

It wasn't. Brady, Nash, Gunner, Asa, and Ryker were all lying around on different chairs or slumped over, asleep in their seats. They hadn't left. Even though I'd asked them all to go home, these five hadn't left. We had been a friends and teammates since we were kids, but more than that . . . we were a family.

"I'm going to go call your grandmother. She'd want to know. You go wake the boys and tell them."

My mother's mother had never come around much. We'd gone to visit her over the years, but she was a stuffy old rich woman who looked down her nose at the life my mother had chosen. My grandfather had passed away of a heart attack when I was five. I didn't remember much about him. They were the only grandparents I had met. My dad's parents had died in a car accident on Old Morphy Bridge in a storm when he was away at college. He'd been an only child just like my mom.

I felt numb. Almost as if it weren't real. As if I were going to go home, and he'd be there waiting on us. Wanting Momma to make meat loaf and asking me about my day.

It was impossible to comprehend that he was really gone.

First I went to Brady, who was slumped in a chair with his baseball cap pulled down over his face. He moved the minute I nudged his shoulder. Shoving his hat back on his head, he looked up at me. I didn't have to say anything. He knew.

Standing up, he pulled me in for a hug. "I'm sorry, man. So damn sorry."

I nodded, and he moved back and helped me wake the others. Each one told me how sorry he was, and that if I needed anything, to call them. They'd do whatever. I thanked them for staying and told them all I'd call when I knew the funeral arrangements.

Brady was the last to follow the others out. He stopped and looked back at me. "Do you want me to wake Maggie and tell her? I can bring her to you if . . . you need me to."

I shook my head. I needed to get my momma home in bed, and Maggie needed her rest. She'd been with me more than seventeen hours yesterday without sleep. "When she wakes up, tell her to call me."

Brady frowned. I'd said for her to call me not text me. He was confused. Thankfully, he didn't question it, just nodded before turning to go.

I let Maggie's words play over and over again in my head, telling me I was strong. I would get through this. Then I went to find Momma and take her home.

After Momma was asleep, I crawled into bed and crashed. The numbness hadn't left me yet. Even with coming home and his not being here, it hadn't fully sunk in. I embraced that for now.

I slept for more than fourteen hours. It was dark outside when I finally opened my eyes. I heard Momma talking to someone and thanking them for the food. Must have been the knock at the front door that woke me.

Getting up, I grabbed a shirt and pulled it on, then headed down the hallway to see how she was doing. I had hoped I would wake up before her. I hadn't meant to sleep all day.

Momma was walking to the kitchen with a casserole dish in her hands. She turned to look at me, and the dark circles under her eyes worried me. "Miriam Lee brought us some dinner. Sweet of her," Momma said, forcing a smile.

Miriam was Nash's mother. She'd always been nice to Momma even if they had never been close friends. Miriam didn't socialize much with the other women in Lawton either. But from the times I'd been to Nash's house, I knew she was a nice lady.

"You gonna eat?" I asked her, hoping she'd say yes. I didn't feel much like eating, but I knew I needed to.

She shrugged then sniffed and wiped at her eyes. "I'm not hungry just yet."

"When was the last time you ate?"

She shrugged again.

I moved around the bar and put my arm around her shoulders, then forced her toward the table. "Sit. You're eating. We both are. We need to eat."

She sat down willingly. I grabbed two plates and dished up some homemade lasagna.

I set the plate in front of her then placed a fork and napkin down beside it before getting us both drinks.

Once I had everything on the table, I sat down at my chair. "He'd want us to eat. I promised him I'd take care of you. Help me keep my promise."

Momma sniffled again then nodded. I waited until she took a bite of her food before eating mine. We ate in silence. The lasagna was really good, and once I started eating, I realized I was starving. I went and made myself another plate before Momma had even forced down half of hers.

"I'm going to take a bath and go back to bed," she said quietly. "I have some of those sleeping pills left. I think I'll take one. I didn't get much sleep today. I can't turn my thoughts off. I can't stop missing him."

I set my second serving down and walked over to kiss her on the head. "We're gonna miss him. We'll always miss him. But we have each other, and we will make it through this." I could hear Maggie's encouragement as the words came out of my mouth. Without her the past three weeks, would I have been able to say that? To help my momma deal? I doubted it.

Momma reached up and patted my arm. "Thank you," she whispered then stood up and headed back down the hallway to her room.

I looked down at my plate, and I wasn't so hungry anymore.

I Take It Back

CHAPTER 29

MAGGIE

I called West as soon as Brady told me the news this morning. But he hadn't answered. I'd texted him twice, but he hadn't replied. I considered walking to his house, which was four miles away, but decided he was probably sleeping.

I waited. All day.

It was after nine that evening when my phone finally rang. I was curled up in my window seat, watching and waiting for some sign of him. His name lit up the screen.

"Hey," I said as I pressed the phone to my ear.

"Hey. Sorry I missed your call and texts. I slept all day. Haven't been up long. Nash's mother brought lasagna over, so I got Momma to eat something. She's gone back to bed now."

"I hoped you were getting sleep. Did you eat too?"

"Yeah. It was good lasagna."

"I'm sorry I left. I should have stayed." All day I had regretted leaving. I shouldn't have let him and my aunt and uncle convince me to go home to sleep. He'd lost his dad, and I hadn't been there for him. But Brady had, and I was glad for that.

"Nothing you could have done. I wanted you to go get your rest. Don't apologize for doing what I asked you to do."

"How's your mom?"

He sighed. "Sad. Missing him."

"How are you?"

He didn't respond at first. I almost wished I hadn't asked that. He'd probably been asked that enough. "I'm in denial, I think. Does that happen? I mean, it's like I keep expecting him to walk through the door any minute. It doesn't seem real."

I knew that feeling. Once I had stopped screaming in a corner, I had gone through a time where I expected my mother to show up at any moment and take me home. Or I'd wake up from the nightmare I was having. "That will fade. When it does, it isn't easy. Right now you're coping."

He didn't say anything at first. We just sat in silence on each end of the phone.

"I've slept all day. I won't be able to sleep tonight. Would you . . . would you sneak out after your aunt and uncle are in bed and go riding with me? I want to get out, but I don't want to be alone."

It was five minutes after eleven when I slipped out my window and went down the fire escape ladder. West was waiting at the bottom so I could jump to him. The ladder didn't go all the way to the ground.

"Let's go," he whispered in my ear, then grabbed my hand. We ran down the driveway to his truck.

I had never snuck out in my life. But doing it for West seemed like the appropriate time to do it. I was finding that I would do anything he asked me to.

West opened the passenger door and helped me up inside before closing it and going over to his side. He kept his headlights off until we had backed out and headed away from my house. When he finally turned them on, he glanced over at me. "Thank you."

The moonlight shone on the emptiness in his eyes, an emptiness I was all too familiar with. That feeling wouldn't go away any time soon. Even when it began to ease, there would be days when he'd wake up and it would hit him again at full force.

I unbuckled my seat belt and moved over to the middle

before fastening it again and sliding my hand over his. I couldn't do anything to make the pain stop. No one could. But I could sit here and let him know he wasn't alone.

West flipped his hand over and threaded his fingers through mine. This connection between us meant something more to me than it did to him, but that didn't matter. At least I got to experience it.

We drove for more than thirty minutes without music or talking. I had no idea where we were going, but as long as I was with West, I didn't care. I did know we had left Lawton behind. If we kept heading this way, we'd be in Tennessee soon.

"I want to show you something," West said as he slowed down and turned off the highway. We drove a few miles before he slowed then turned again. This road was unpaved and narrow. It was between tall trees, and spooky at night.

When the trees cleared, we were on a bluff overlooking a small town with only a few lights still on. West opened the truck door and stepped out, then reached for my hand. "Come on," he said with a smile on his lips. I would have gone anywhere to get him to smile on a day like today.

I took his hand and moved to climb out on his side. West grabbed my waist and picked me up instead of letting me get down on my own. I wasn't going to complain. His hands lingered a moment longer than necessary, and I couldn't help but wish we were something more. That West was mine. Because whether he realized it or not, I was his.

I followed him as close to the edge as I was willing to get. I wasn't afraid of heights, but I wasn't about to go out on the edge of a bluff.

"That's Lawton. Looks so small from up here. Peaceful. There's no pain from up here. No loss."

I moved my gaze from the town to look at West.

He had his hands tucked into the front pockets of his jeans as he stared down. The moonlight only made him even more beautiful.

"Dad used to bring me here when I was a kid. Told me that I would be the biggest thing to come out of Lawton. That I could do whatever I set my mind to. I loved looking down on my town and realizing I was standing over it, larger than it was. Or so it seemed." He paused and let out a sad laugh. "But without Dad here, I don't want that dream anymore. I don't care about being the biggest thing to come out of Lawton. Truth is, the biggest thing to come out of Lawton will be Brady. I just want to survive, to forget, to remember."

"You'll survive and you'll remember, but you're never going to forget. One day you'll be thankful for those memories. Thankful you don't forget."

West turned to look at me then. The anguish in his gaze made my throat tighten and my chest ache. "Only you. Only you, Maggie. I can't imagine being able to let anyone else close to me. I've never been one to let people in. But something about you has gotten to me since the first moment I saw you. I just—" He shook his head as if he didn't know what to say. "I can't figure out how to handle it. You. What I'm feeling."

"Do you remember the first time we met?" I asked him, unable to let it go. I wanted him to admit he remembered kissing me. Maybe I shouldn't push that tonight, but at least it was a distraction. He needed that too.

A small smile tugged on his lips, and he looked away from me, back down at the town below us. "Yeah. Not exactly something a guy forgets."

Okay. . . . Did that mean he remembered kissing me? Or that I didn't used to talk?

"You've never mentioned that night," I said, wanting more from him.

He turned his gaze back to me. "But I think about it all the time. Even though I shouldn't. I think about it."

That made me happy. Knowing he liked remembering that moment. Because it was one of my favorite memories, and I wanted him to think about it too.

"Do you think about it?" he asked.

I nodded but didn't say anything else.

He took a step toward me, and my heart rate picked up. "Do you think about it often?"

If he got any closer, I wasn't sure I would be able to continue breathing. The birds in my stomach were going crazy. Finally I nodded.

"Did you enjoy it?" he asked.

Oh God. I needed air. Lots of air. West was so close to me now, and he was asking me if I had enjoyed our kiss. I managed a nod, then blurted out, "Did you?" before I could stop myself.

He grinned. "Best I ever had."

I stared up at him and held his gaze. "It was the only one I've ever had."

West froze, and his sexy smolder turned to surprise. "What?" he asked.

I wanted him to know he was my first kiss. My only kiss. It was special to me. I wanted it to be special to him, too. "That was the first kiss I ever had. The only kiss I've ever had."

West held my gaze as he looked at me with disbelief. Then he hung his head and muttered a curse before backing away from me. That was definitely not the reaction I'd wanted.

I wasn't sure how to fix this. I was good at helping him

deal with pain and sorrow because that was something I knew. I didn't know much about boy-girl relationships.

I had just opened my mouth to say something when West lifted his face and turned back to me. Then he moved. I didn't have a chance to react before his hands were on my waist and his chest was pressed against mine. "A girl's first kiss should never be from an asshole who's taking his anger at life out on her. Lips this sweet shouldn't be treated the way I treated them. I can't take it back, but I can replace it. With something better." He dipped his head. "This is what your first kiss should have been like," he whispered against my lips before his mouth covered mine.

His hands moved to cup my face as if I were something he treasured and didn't want to break. Then his tongue slid across my bottom lip, and I opened up for him.

My hands slid into his hair as I held on to him. The warmth of his minty breath teased me and made me crave more. When the tip of his tongue slid along mine, I trembled in his arms.

His hands moved down from my face and grabbed my waist again as he jerked me closer to him and deepened the kiss. It was as if he couldn't get enough of me. Not like I was any better. My hands fisted in his hair and were holding him to me. Afraid he'd leave me again. I wasn't sure I could handle him regretting this. I didn't want him to pretend like this hadn't happened.

I heard a distant moan and realized it had come from me. West broke our kiss. He didn't move far, just rested his forehead against mine while breathing heavily. "I take it back. This . . . this was the best I've ever had."

My body hummed with pleasure. I had made him feel this way. Me. His friend. The girl he didn't touch that way or look at with any kind of attraction.

I Would Not Lose Her

CHAPTER 30

WEST

I had just wanted to fix it. Make her first kiss something special. I didn't want that kiss I'd taken while I was hurting to be her first fucking kiss. I just meant to give her what she deserved. But holy hell, she'd tasted even better than I remembered. Her body was meant to be worshiped. It molded so perfectly under my hands. And her sweet sounds. God help me, I wanted more of that. Of her.

Fuck.

I hadn't meant to do that. What we had was more than this. More than a sexual attraction. More than something cheap. It was deeper, and I couldn't lose it. If I had more with her, I would mess it up and I would lose her. But I couldn't lose

Maggie. I would do anything to keep her. Including not taking more of that mouth currently swollen and wet from my kiss.

"West?" she whispered. I could hear the unease in her voice.

I forced my hands to let her go.

"That . . . that was how it should have been," I said, forcing myself to look at her but not grab her again.

Maggie touched her lips with her fingertips, and I swear to God my knees buckled a little. She had to stop doing sexy shit.

Her eyes were studying me. The endearing, glazed-over look they'd had when I'd first moved away from her was turning into something else. I was confusing her. Damn it.

"I wanted your first kiss to be special, Maggie. That was all," I said, hearing the lie in my own voice.

Her hand dropped to her side, and her gaze fell to the ground. "It was. Both of them. In different ways," she said without looking at me.

Was she hurt? Why wasn't she looking at me?

"Are you okay? Did I do something I shouldn't have? Don't be mad at me. I didn't mean to upset you."

She lifted her gaze and gave me a smile that didn't meet her eyes. There was sadness to it. "You didn't do anything wrong. I'm not upset. Just taken by surprise. But not upset . . . Thank you."

We didn't talk about it again. I led us back to the truck, and Maggie sat beside me as we looked out at the town. We talked some but not much. This was all I needed. Having her here with me. When I was alone, I'd let myself remember how she felt in my arms. How she tasted and the sounds she made that drove me crazy. But for now I was just thankful I had her with me.

Around three that morning I got Maggie safely back up to her room before heading home. Momma was sleeping peacefully. I was sure the pill had helped. I thought about taking a shower, but I took a sniff of my shirt. I could smell the faint scent of vanilla. I decided I wouldn't shower or even change.

I climbed into bed and went to sleep thinking about Maggie. I held on to memories of that kiss to keep the other memories back. I wasn't ready to face them yet.

The next day was full, helping Momma make funeral arrangements. Dad had left several requests about his funeral. It was tough reading the paper where he'd written them down. Several times I reached for my phone, wanting to hear Maggie's voice. But I never dialed.

I had to be strong for my mother today. I couldn't keep reaching out for Maggie.

Making sure my momma ate and slept took all my attention while I answered the door and took in the food people in town were bringing. Where they thought we'd put all this, I didn't know. We had more food than we had space. I filled up the freezer and fridge. Now things were just sitting on the bar. For the last pound cake that had arrived, I'd just put it on the table.

Why did they think food would help? Getting my mother to actually eat was hard enough. I sure couldn't eat all this by myself.

The funeral was scheduled for three days after Dad's passing. Dealing with the arrangements, the phone calls, and my mother had kept me from talking to Maggie for more than an hour the past couple of nights. I hadn't been to school this week, and I didn't make the mistake of going to get her. I was so emotional right now, I couldn't be sure I wouldn't kiss her again. Pull her closer. My need for her was changing and growing, and I was scared of it. I didn't trust myself to push things further with her and not mess up. I always messed up.

I would not lose her.

I Wish I Had Been There
CHAPTER 31

MAGGIE

I didn't wear black. There would be enough black. Enough sadness. I didn't remember much about my mother's funeral. The only thing I did remember was the black. I hated all the black. My mother hated black. She said it was drab. Everyone needed some color in their life.

Jude wouldn't have liked all the black either. He'd liked to laugh, and he'd looked for the brightness in life. I chose a green dress that matched my eyes. Because he'd said my eyes were pretty.

Uncle Boone, Aunt Coralee, Brady, and I all rode together to the graveside ceremony. Most funerals in the South were held in churches or funeral homes before they took the casket to the grave. But West said his dad hadn't wanted a long ceremony for people to mourn. He wanted it quick. Easy. Nothing fancy.

We parked along the street like everyone else and then made our way to the large white tent where people were beginning to gather. I searched for West until our eyes met. He was standing by his mother, watching me walk toward him. Today would be the day it would finally become real to him.

My mother's funeral hadn't been when it had sunk in for me, simply because I hadn't been well then. My mind had been refusing to accept what I had witnessed. But I knew seeing his father lowered into the ground would hit West hard. And I would be there if he needed me.

West motioned for me to come stand beside him. I didn't glance back at my aunt and uncle to make sure it was okay. I knew they'd understand. I walked past the rows of people until I was close enough for West to take my hand in his. The firm grip told me he wasn't okay.

"I like your dress," he said, leaning down to whisper near my ear. "It matches your eyes."

I glanced up at him. "Your dad liked my eyes. He said they were pretty."

A sad smile touched his lips. "Yeah, he did. He'd like that dress, too."

Others arrived and came to say their condolences to West and his mother. Through it all he never let go of my hand. When the minister began speaking, West's mother sank into the chair placed behind her and sobbed quietly.

I could feel West tremble beside me when it was time for him to lay the rose on his father's casket. I eased my hand out of his and waited as he walked forward and put the red rose down. "You'll always be my hero," he said, loud enough that I could hear him, as he stared at the casket.

When he turned and walked back to me, I could see the tense expression on his face. He was holding back the emotion I knew was strangling him while trying to stay strong for his mother.

His hand was back in mine the moment he was beside me.

I didn't hear much that was said after that. I was too focused on West and the rigid way he was standing. It was as if he'd turned to stone. His grip on my hand was like he was holding on to me for fear I'd run off.

I was okay with that. I didn't intend to leave him.

As the casket began to lower into the grave, West inhaled sharply, and his mother stood up and grabbed on to his arm, leaning into him. He wrapped his arm around his momma and held her against him.

Slowly, people began to leave. Some came by and patted West on the back and said something to his mother, but it was all very quiet. Brady, Asa, Nash, Gunner, and Ryker all walked up and stood behind West. Each one squeezed his shoulder and said things like, "I'm here if you need me, man," and "Love you, bro," and "You need me, call me."

West nodded and acknowledged all of them. Each one also stopped and hugged Olivia, which only made her cry more. Once they were done, they all slowly walked away. I didn't know what West wanted me to do, but I knew my aunt and uncle were waiting on me.

I looked up at him. "I'll stay if you need me."

He glanced over at his mother, then back at me. "Can you get out tonight?"

I could do whatever he wanted me to do. I nodded.

"I'll be at the bottom of the ladder at eleven."

"I'll meet you there."

There was a knock on my bedroom door around ten that night. I knew my aunt and uncle were already in bed, so the only person it could be was Brady. I had stayed up here the rest of the day and tried to read. But my mind had been on West and his mother. If he needed me and called, I wanted to be alone so I could answer him.

Opening the door to Brady, I stared up at him curiously. He never came to my room. He barely even tried talking to me anymore. I couldn't blame him. It was hard to talk to someone who didn't talk back.

"Can I come in?" he asked.

I nodded, stepping back so he could come in. Again, something he never did. I knew this was about West. I imagined Brady had been worrying about him today too. It was hard not to after the last few days.

Brady walked in, his hands tucked into his front pockets, looking unsure of what to do or say.

"Mom and Dad are asleep, but sound travels down that hall. Could you close the door?" he asked.

I did as he asked.

"I saw you talk to him today. I thought I saw it before, but I definitely know I saw it today."

I had expected this, eventually. Although I had tried not talking to him where people could see, there were times like today when I hadn't worried about anything other than comforting West.

I didn't reply. What did he want me to say? Did he expect me to admit it and talk to him? Because that would change everything. Tomorrow I'd have to face a life where people expected me to talk. They'd invade my privacy and want to know things I didn't want to tell them.

Not talking was my security blanket. I wasn't ready to let it go.

"I didn't see it once, Maggie. I saw it several times. And I've seen it at school. You don't always move your mouth, but West is listening to you. I can tell by his expression." Brady sighed and ran a hand through his hair. "I'm not here to demand that you talk to me. Or anyone. I'm just . . . I'm confused. If you can talk, why wouldn't you talk to everyone? Why just West?"

He was asking questions. Questions he wanted me to answer with my voice. But I wouldn't talk, not tonight. I walked over to get the note pad on my window seat. I wrote:

He needs me. I understand him and his pain.

Then I handed the pad to Brady.

He read it then lifted his eyes back to me. "So, this is your connection. This is why he's with you all the time and he's all of the sudden holding your hand and acting like he needs you to breathe. He wasn't lying about you just being friends. You're helping him deal with all . . . this."

I nodded.

Brady looked relieved. He held the note pad out for me. "I get it. But one day you'll need to focus on helping you. Hiding from the world this way isn't healthy. You're not healing. You're avoiding."

No, I was protecting myself. I didn't write that down, though. I just stood and waited for him to leave or say something else.

My phone dinged, and I reached into my pocket for it.

I'm outside. Waiting on you at the bottom of the ladder.

He was here. I glanced at the window then back at Brady.

"He's out there, isn't he?" Brady said, following my gaze to the window.

I could lie, but I trusted Brady. He loved West too.

So I nodded.

He gave me a sad smile. "Be careful, Maggie."

He had said that before. Many times. I had told myself that too. But it no longer seemed to matter. I was past the point of being careful where West was concerned, and I didn't know how to fix that. Or if I even wanted to.

I waited until he'd left my room then closed the door behind him and hurried to the window to climb out.

It Was Selfish, But I Did It Anyway
CHAPTER 32

WEST

The reality of my father's death had exploded in my chest the moment they lowered him into the ground. In that moment it became real. Maggie had been right. It wasn't a pain you could describe and nothing could ease it.

Momma cried all afternoon as I held her. Finally I got her to take a sleeping pill and go to bed. I had been strong for her as long as I could. I had to break down too. But selfishly, I wanted Maggie with me when I did. If she were there, I wouldn't lose myself to the pain. She'd keep me from falling.

Staring up at her window, I watched as she opened it

and climbed out. Today she hadn't asked me stupid stuff like "Are you okay?" or "Is there anything I can do?" She was just there. Silently giving me strength.

When she started coming down the ladder, I put my hands on either side to steady it and stood beneath her in case she fell.

I didn't need to talk. I just wanted her to go with me and be there as I sat in silence. Maggie would do that. It was one of the reasons she was so damn special.

"Let's go," I whispered when she was at the bottom, and then I led her back to the truck.

Maggie didn't slide over beside me when she got in. I wanted her to, but I didn't push it. She did it before because she'd wanted to. Our friendship line was getting blurred, and I knew it. I just wasn't sure how to stop it. And tonight I didn't want to stop it.

We drove without music or talking until we got to the bluff. I cut the engine and lights and just sat there. The lights from the town reminded me of Dad. The sharp pain hit me as I thought about the fact that he would never come up here again, would never sit in my truck and laugh at my driving again. He'd never . . . He'd never see me graduate. He wouldn't be there when I got married. He wouldn't be my kids' grandfather.

My throat tightened, and I punched the steering wheel several times, trying to release some of my pain. He was gone. Forever. I'd never see my dad again.

Maggie was beside me, and her small hand covered one of mine. There was nothing to say. If her father were put on death row, she'd go through another version of this. At least now he was in prison. She knew he was breathing. He was there, even if she didn't want to see him again.

"Do you have days when all you think about are the things she'll never see in your life?" I asked her.

"Yeah. All the time," she replied.

She was living this hell too. I chanted that over and over to myself, proving I wasn't the only one. I began to relax enough to let go of the intense grip I had on the steering wheel.

In that moment I made a decision. I didn't care about the line. I didn't care about protecting our friendship. I just needed Maggie. I needed to feel her and forget all of this. I knew I was being selfish, but I had to do it anyway.

Turning, I slid a hand into her hair and covered her mouth with mine. I gave her a moment to decide. If she didn't want this, she'd push me away.

But she didn't. I'd known deep down, she wouldn't. I knew she felt this between us too.

With each brush of her hand on my skin, I grew desperate. I wanted more of her. So when she leaned closer to me, I placed my hands on her hips and moved us both over to the passenger side. My thumbs grazed her bare skin as her arms wrapped around my neck and the shirt she was wearing lifted an inch.

Maggie shivered in my arms, causing my heart to pump even faster. She liked this as much as I did. The look in her eyes said everything I was feeling.

"Lift your arms, Maggie," I instructed, not asking.

Without hesitation, she lifted her arms and let me take her shirt off. The delicate creamy skin of her shoulders made her look like an angel.

She closed her eyes and inhaled sharply when I slid the straps down her arms then pulled the bra away from her. "You're beautiful," I said breathlessly.

Leaning closer, I pressed a kiss to her neck, and she swallowed hard. Her hands came up to grip my shoulders as if she needed to hold on. I liked that. No, I fucking loved that. I wanted her to hold on to me. To trust me.

With great control, I slowly kissed a path downward. She was watching me, her mouth slightly open. I'd never felt this close to anyone before.

"West," Maggie whispered my name as her hands gripped my arms tightly.

This was going to be my undoing. This girl. She was going to claim me.

CHAPTER 33

MAGGIE

He was hurting. I had to remember that. He was lost and hurting and seeking comfort. I should stop him. I shouldn't let him do something he'd regret tomorrow.

But I couldn't.

He looked at me like he wanted me desperately. Like he wanted this desperately. Like I was beautiful.

I cracked a little more.

I'd never felt like this; my body hadn't known it could feel like this. And I was enjoying this too much to make him stop.

"West," I managed to get out. But I quickly forgot why I'd even said his name as his kisses moved lower.

My head was spinning. I wasn't getting enough oxygen. Or maybe I was getting too much. I didn't know. I just wanted more of him. Of this.

His hand settled firmly on my back, pressing my bare chest against his as his mouth covered mine again. "You feel so damn good," he whispered as he nibbled and licked at my lips. I agreed, he felt just as good.

I got so lost in his embrace, at first I didn't notice that his fingertips were grazing the inner waistband of my shorts.

I wanted to believe he wanted me. But I feared he just needed anyone right now. If it were Raleigh here, would he want her? Was this just a distraction and I was simply the available girl?

I felt a pain in my chest at the thought. I didn't want to be just a distraction. He meant too much to me for that to be all I was to him. But how did I tell him no when he was hurting so much?

"West," I choked out, and he froze. That got his attention fast.

He dropped his head to my shoulder and breathed deeply. He didn't move his hand. "No one has made me feel the way you do, Maggie."

I didn't have anyone to compare this to, but I doubted anyone would ever make me feel the way West did.

He continued in a hoarse whisper, "Being with you . . . having you . . . I dream about it. It's something I can't explain and I can't lose, either."

That was it. What I needed to hear.

"Okay," I replied, knowing I'd never regret this with him.

He lifted his head, and those blue eyes flared with heat. I was trembling even before his hand slid down farther.

"Trust me?" His voice was thick and raspy.

I just nodded. I couldn't speak.

My heart was pounding so loudly, I could hear it. My body was on fire, about to shatter into a beautiful oblivion.

I'd said I'd be whatever he needed. I'd do whatever he needed me to do.

I knew now I had been so very right.

He slowly lifted his head and gazed down at me. "I need you. No, I want you. Just you. I don't need or want anything else." When he opened his eyes, they were glassy, and I could see the emotion he was holding back.

"What do you want from me?" I asked.

"I need you too much. I want you so much. You're just . . . I just . . . You're the only thing that makes the pain go away, Maggie."

He was trying to survive. I was giving him a reason to survive. He was taking from me. But I wanted to give myself to him.

I ran my hands over his hair and tried to comfort him. I knew he wasn't ready to hear me tell him I loved him. I wasn't sure he'd ever want to hear that. But I had to tell him a small portion of the truth.

"I want this. I want you like this. Don't apologize. What you're taking, I am giving you willingly."

He didn't reply at first. When he finally lifted his head, I saw the heat in his eyes as he looked at me. "I want more. More than I deserve."

I couldn't imagine that, years from now, I'd looked back on this night and regret it. Even if this were it for us, I'd have been completely connected with West. It may have been a way to help him with his pain, but it also helped me with mine. Watching him lose his father brought back so much heartache and loss for me. The moments we had just shared made me feel alive. More alive than I'd felt in a very long time.

"I want more too," I replied.

My heart started to flutter at the idea, and West's sharp intake of breath told me he understood exactly what I was telling him.

"I don't want to be a regret for you. Ever," he said, looking torn.

"And I don't want to be a regret for you. Ever," I repeated back to him. I wanted him to cherish this memory just like I would. I wanted to be more to him. Something he'd never forget.

"Nothing about any moment I've spent with you will ever be a regret." The fierceness on his face made me shiver. I felt special. He made me feel that way.

Just. To. Me.

CHAPTER 34

WEST

Nothing in life had prepared me for this. My heart felt like it was going to beat right out of my body.

I shed the rest of my clothes after taking a condom out of my pocket. I was so nervous, my hands shook as I put it on.

As I lowered my body over hers, my chest tightened. Finally those eyes I'd come to dream about lifted to meet mine. There was a quiet confidence there. A trust I would cherish. One I couldn't lose.

With careful ease, I entered her, and she held on to me through it all. Never taking her eyes off mine.

* * *

Later, when she curled up against me in the truck and I held her while I looked out at the lights of Lawton below us, I let the first tear fall.

For all that I had lost.

For all that I had found.

For all I couldn't lose now but feared I would.

The next day I returned to school. My mother's mom would be arriving today, and I didn't want to be there. Why mother had called her and asked her to come, I didn't know. She'd never been around us much before.

Of course I also wanted to see Maggie.

Taking her home last night, I'd been so scared of losing her that I'd been dead silent. Too silent. Rather than my own thoughts, my concern should have been Maggie. I would fix that today.

The one thing I didn't want to face was people telling me they were sorry to hear about my dad. I didn't want to think about it. I also didn't want them looking at me with pity. So I ignored everyone as I walked through the doors and headed straight for my locker.

Maggie was standing there, her books tucked close to her chest, waiting. A warmth spread through me that only Maggie could cause, and I hurried through the crowd to get to her. When she spotted me, her lips curled into a small smile. It said so many things. It was for me. She didn't give that smile to anyone else.

I liked that. I liked that a whole fucking lot.

"Morning," I said as I reached her and tugged her close to me before pressing a kiss to those lips that were smiling just for me.

She tensed at first but quickly melted into me and let me have a taste. I didn't want anyone else seeing how good she looked with those swollen lips, so I pulled away after I got enough to get me through first period. Still, I kept my hand on her back and pressed her close to me.

"Ah, good morning," she replied, looking flustered.

Grinning, I pressed a kiss to her nose. "God, you're always so damn pretty," I said.

Her cheeks flushed pink, and she ducked her head as a grin spread across her lips.

"I didn't think you'd come today," she said as she glanced up at me.

Me neither. Until I'd woken up thinking about her. Maggie was here, and this was where I wanted to be. With her.

"You're here," I admitted. She needed to know how I felt. Even if I wasn't sure exactly what that was just yet.

"West," she said breathlessly, and reached up to tuck

a strand of hair behind her ear. "I wish we had classes together."

So did I. Next semester I'd make sure we did. I hated not getting to see her except at lunch and in the halls.

"You're talking." Brady's voice startled us both.

Maggie's eyes went wide as she stared up at me. She wasn't turning to look at him. There was a panic in her green depths, and a protectiveness came over me. I moved her closer to me and slightly behind as I faced Brady.

"Not to you. Not to anyone else. So back off, and keep your mouth shut." I held his gaze and let him read into that whatever the hell he wanted to. Because I wasn't giving her up. Everyone needed to know she was mine now. Including Brady.

"What . . . but she doesn't talk. If she can talk or is talking again, then—"

"Just to me, Brady. Get that. Just. To. Me."

He moved his eyes to her, and I could see frustration there, but I also knew he was my best friend. I'd buried my dad yesterday. He had to give me some slack. For now. I knew we'd have to deal with him eventually.

He finally let out a frustrated sigh. "Fine. But others are going to notice. I just did."

Then he turned and left. Maggie didn't move from where I had tucked her behind me.

He was right. If she weren't careful, others would see her. How did I protect her from that? Not everyone would back down like Brady had.

Especially his parents.

CHAPTER 35

MAGGIE

I could feel Brady watching me all morning. It was a reminder not to speak where I could be seen. But it made me wonder: What would happen if West wasn't the only person I spoke to? Would this end? Would he feel as if he didn't have a special part of me anymore?

"You must be fucking him now." I recognized Raleigh's voice even before turning around to face her. I had gone to the restroom to wash my hands before lunch.

I glanced up into the mirror to see her glaring back at me with hatred. "It'll end when he's over his grieving. He's using you to get through this thing with his dad. You don't talk, so he likes it. Now you're fucking him. He must like his girls silent when he fucks them now."

I dried my hands on a paper towel then headed for the door. I wasn't going to stand there and take it.

"When he's over this, when he isn't hurting over his dad, he'll come back to me. We have a thing. He loves me. He just couldn't deal."

I continued ignoring her, and opened the door.

"He used to tell me he loved me when he was fucking me. Said I made him feel incredible. Nothing would ever be that good. Bet he doesn't tell you he loves you, does he?" she said as I walked out the door.

I was glad I hadn't been facing her when she'd said that. Because then she'd have seen the answer on my face.

As wonderful as my time with West had been last night, he never told me he loved me. He didn't say much at all. When it was over, he held me to him. I enjoyed being in his arms. The one tear he'd let fall was, I believed, him dealing with his grief.

But maybe it had been about more than that.

Maybe I had been a mistake.

"There you are." West's voice always made my heart rate pick up. And especially now, with me worrying that maybe he did love Raleigh, I was happy he was here.

I glanced over to see him walking toward me. A frown touched his face as he got closer. "What's wrong?" he asked when he reached me.

His hand cupped my face. I loved when he did that. It made me feel safe. Like his large hands could protect me.

The restroom door opened behind me, and I felt him tense. Oh God, he still reacted to her. He had loved her. I hadn't known he had loved her. The feeling of safety left me, and I shook my head in answer to his question while simultaneously moving away from her. Away from him. Away from my confused emotions.

"Did you do that? Is she upset because you said something to her?" West was angry. I turned to see him glaring at Raleigh much the same way she'd glared at me. His glare was just more intense. And frightening.

Raleigh shrugged and flipped her dark hair over her shoulder as if nothing had happened. "I've moved on, West. I don't care who you do," she snapped at him before strutting away. I knew she didn't mean what she'd said, but she was a great actress.

"She said something to you," he said, closing the distance between us again.

I shrugged. "Nothing much. She's just . . . not over you."

He slid his hand over my hip. "Whatever she said, don't listen to her. She's trying to hurt me, and she's figured out that hurting you will hurt me. That's all."

I didn't think he was right about that, but I wasn't going to correct him. Instead I changed the subject.

"I thought you'd be eating by now," I said.

He smirked, then bent his head to kiss my lips once. "Not without you."

Oh. I didn't know what to think about that. What were we now? Had last night really changed us?

He put his hand on my back. "Come on. Let's go eat."

I went. Because I had no idea how to ask him what we were now.

"Missed you this morning," he said, his hand not leaving me.

"We texted." I reminded him of the many texts he'd sent me throughout morning classes.

"Can't see your face in a text," he replied.

The birds in my stomach woke up.

When we got to the cafeteria door, West reached in front of us and opened it, and we walked inside together.

Every eye in the place was on us . . . or it felt like it. I could feel people staring. Wondering what had happened with us. Why our friendship seemed more intimate now. I glanced over at his table, and Brady, Asa, and Ryker were all watching us. Gunner was the only one who didn't find us entertaining. He was too busy glaring at his phone while he texted something.

I didn't look at anyone else as we walked through the line. West's arm went around my shoulders, and he tugged me close to him as he placed a kiss to my temple. Surprised, I glanced up at him, but suddenly he was looking at someone else with a scowl. Following his gaze, I saw that Nash had stopped to watch us, his tray in his hands.

Nash looked at me, then shook his head and walked off toward the table with the other guys. I was sure they'd seen that interaction between West and Nash. Would Brady make it okay with them now that West and I were . . . doing whatever this was?

"Is he mad?" I whispered. I didn't want his friends upset with him. He needed their support right now.

"Don't care. If he is, he'll get over it."

That wasn't the answer I was hoping for.

He grabbed my tray and his, and we walked over to the table and our vacant seats in between Brady and Nash.

West sat down next to Nash, which was normally where I sat. He was making a statement today. I just wasn't sure what it was yet.

"So, y'all are a thing now?" Gunner asked, dropping his phone onto the table and reaching for his soda. "Thought she was off-limits and shit."

"Don't," Brady said before West could react. "This ain't got nothing to do with you."

Gunner seemed more amused than anything. He picked

up his apple and smirked. "Sure don't." Then he glanced at Nash before taking a bite and grinning.

I wanted to be anywhere but here.

"I was wondering, though, Maggie. You got a date for the homecoming dance yet?" Gunner asked.

"Gunner, shit, man," Ryker muttered.

I didn't look up. I studied the fries I was about to eat and pretended like I didn't hear him. I hadn't thought about the homecoming dance. I'd seen the posters and I'd heard the announcements, but I wasn't thinking about it. I'd never been to a dance. I didn't expect to go to this one.

"She's with me, Gunner. She's going with me. Every-where," West replied. "Is that enough clarification for you?"

His hand slid over my knee and squeezed as he spoke.

"Well, that clears that up," Asa said with a chuckle. "We gonna let this slide or what?"

I glanced up at Asa to see who he was talking to. His gaze was fixed on Brady.

My cousin simply nodded. Nothing else was said.

Talk of Friday's game began to take over, and I eventually relaxed enough to eat most of my lunch.

She Had Become My Everything
CHAPTER 36

WEST

Coach had said I didn't have to be at practice this week. Although, if I wanted to, I could still play in the game. He knew they needed me, and he also knew my dad would have wanted me to play. So, I'd play.

I had missed all the other practices, but I wasn't going to miss this one. My grandmother was at my house by now, so I knew my mother wasn't alone. It gave me some freedom, but it also was keeping me from my house. I didn't want that woman there. She'd never visited, not once my entire life. We always had to go to her home. She rarely spoke to my father or acknowledged him.

I felt nothing for her.

But my mother loved her.

No one questioned me when I walked into the locker room to get my practice gear on. Some nodded, a few slapped me on the back, but no one said a thing. This was what I needed. If I couldn't have Maggie with me all the time, then this was the only other way to keep my mind free of shit.

As I tied my cleats, I stood up to see Brady walking over to me. He wanted answers, and I wasn't going to give them to him. What I'd told him this morning was his answer.

"How long has she been talking to you?" he asked in a hushed voice.

I grabbed my helmet and started walking to the door. "A while," I replied.

"How long's 'a while'? Since the hospital . . . or before?"

"Before."

Brady fell into step beside me. "That's why you grew attached so fast, isn't it? She's been helping you deal with things. She's been there."

I didn't reply. I didn't know the answer. Maybe that was why I'd grown attached to her so quickly. Grief changed you. Made you react differently. But I didn't want to say that I wouldn't have wanted Maggie had she not spoken to me.

But would I have?

"You understand probably better than anyone what

she's gone through. If she's told you stuff, it's more than she's told anyone else."

He was right. She had, but I wasn't going to tell him that.

"She needs to talk to other people," Brady added.

He wasn't going to let up about this. I had to shut this down. Until Maggie was ready to talk, I wasn't going to let anyone make her.

I stopped walking and looked at him. "She isn't ready. It's how she deals. Let her deal with things the way she needs to. I won't let anyone push her. Not even you," I told him. Then I walked off toward the field and left him standing there.

It was almost midnight when Maggie slid her window open for me to come inside. I had practice until late then gone to the bluff and sat up there for a few hours. When Momma had called about me coming home to eat, I did. For her. Then my grandmother had asked me about college, and I had left without answering her. She hadn't been there for us before, and she had no right to interfere with my life now.

I called Momma and told her to go to sleep. Told her I'd be home soon, that I was at Brady's. That was the truth. I was at Brady's. I just wasn't here for Brady. I think she probably knew that, but she didn't ask.

Maggie stood in the middle of her room in a pair of

baggy sweatpants tied at the waist and a tank top. Her long hair was in a messy knot on top of her head, and she couldn't have looked more beautiful. I'd missed her this afternoon. I always missed her when she wasn't with me.

That scared me if I thought about it too much. I didn't want to miss her like this. I could lose her.

No.

I wasn't going to lose Maggie. I wouldn't let that happen. I would make her want to stay with me. I'd be whatever she needed me to be.

"Hey," she said softly.

I grinned. "Hey."

Closing the distance between us, I reached for her and held her close to me. "Missed you," I whispered before pressing a kiss to her lips. She had great lips.

She laughed against my kiss. I loved that sound. She didn't laugh often. But when she did, it was like magic. "What's so funny?" I asked, unable to keep the incredibly pleased smile from hearing her laughter off my face.

"You just saw me a few hours ago," she said.

I shook my head. "No, I saw you nine hours ago. That is not a few. It's a fucking long time."

Maggie pressed her lips together, and her eyes danced with laughter. She wasn't wearing any makeup. Her face was washed clean. I loved that she had known I was coming over and didn't fix up. She was just her, and she was comfortable being just her.

"You really should be sleeping. You have the game tomorrow night," she said as she placed a hand on my chest.

"I am gonna sleep. Here with you. I'll set my alarm to get up at five, and I'll go home. But tonight I want to hold you."

Her eyes sparked with pleasure. That made me think about things. Things I shouldn't be thinking about. Not in her house. Not where Boone was so close to us.

I glanced over at her bed and could see she had already been in it tonight. I hadn't texted her I was coming over until about an hour ago. I wondered if she'd been asleep then. Seeing her covers messy and knowing I was going to have her cuddled up against me all night made everything that felt hollow fade away. Maggie made me feel like a caveman. I liked having her with me.

Maggie slipped her hand into mine, and I had that familiar feeling of peace that had gotten me through this last month. Four weeks. Tomorrow it would have been exactly one month since I kissed her at the field party. She'd come into my life when I thought I was going to lose myself. When I wasn't sure I had the strength to make it. And she'd shown me I could. She had reminded me that I wasn't the only person on earth to lose a parent.

Maggie pulled the covers back on my side then crawled over to her side to straighten her sheets. Seeing her like this, being here with her like this, made me want things. Things that should be for me and me only. For example, I never wanted another guy to see her dressed like that on this bed. Just me. I didn't want her to ever slip her hand in another guy's hand. Ever. Just mine.

"You have to get in in order to go to sleep," Maggie whispered, a playful smile on her lips.

She had become my lifeline. I wanted to be hers. I wanted her to feel this way about me, too.

I climbed into the bed and lay on my back with one arm behind my head and the other one held out for Maggie, inviting her to come lay her head on my chest. She didn't need instruction. She knew exactly what I wanted. When her head was right where I liked it, I slipped my hands into her silky hair and untied her bun. She didn't protest.

We lay there quietly for a few minutes while I played with her hair and stared at the ceiling fan. My head was a mix of emotions. She'd entered my life when I'd needed her most. I'd never expected this. Or her. But now that I had her, I wasn't sure how I'd made it this long without her.

CHAPTER 37

MAGGIE

When Aunt Coralee knocked on my bedroom door to wake me, I had a brief moment of panic until I saw West wasn't in my bed anymore. I guess I hadn't woken up when he'd left.

There was a note on the pillow where he had slept. I rubbed the sleep out of my eyes and then opened the folded paper.

Good morning, beautiful. You were sleeping so peacefully when I left. I didn't want to wake you. But today I'd like to be the one to take you to school. I'll be by at seven thirty. If Brady gives you a hard time, call me and hand the phone to him.

He wanted me to ride with him to school. I glanced up at the mirror across from my bed and saw the smile on my face. It was a real smile, one filled with excitement and hope. For a long time that smile had been a stranger to me. Now I was happy.

Standing up, I walked over to the mirror, then reached out and touched the girl there. She was older than the one I once knew. Her eyes held more strength and maturity. But she was happy. That was familiar.

"You'd like him, Mom," I whispered. "He's wonderful."

She would have wanted me to tell her everything about him. She'd squeal with me when I told her about our first kiss. She would listen to me talk about him and not get bored. She hadn't just been my mother; she'd been my best friend. Knowing that West would make her happy for me made me feel even more complete. The emptiness that had become part of me wasn't so empty anymore. West was filling it.

Aunt Coralee's voice calling that breakfast was ready reminded me that I had to hurry. I wanted to let her know I was riding with West today. It was his game day, and I wanted to surprise him with my school spirit too.

I just needed to get Brady to lend me a jersey.

Fifteen minutes later I was dressed and headed to the kitchen. I had texted Brady asking him if I could borrow a jersey. He'd agreed and said he'd bring it to the kitchen for me. I also had a note in my hand that wasn't asking, more like telling, Aunt Coralee that I was riding with West today.

When I got there, Brady was already at the table eating a plate full of eggs and bacon. He was wearing the blue jersey that he would wear tonight. There was another blue one folded up on the table that had his same number but looked like it had been worn more.

"Here you go. You can take my jersey from last year," he said, a grin tugging on the corners of his lips.

Did he think it was silly for me to wear it? Was this something I shouldn't do yet?

"Good morning, Maggie. I have your plate on the warmer. Let me get it." Aunt Coralee paused and looked at the white tank top I was wearing and frowned. "Um, I don't think you can wear that to school."

"Oh, she's not. She's wearing my old jersey today," he replied.

Aunt Coralee's eyes lit up, and she smiled. "Well, that is so sweet! Isn't it, Brady?"

Brady continued to look like he was going to burst into laughter at any minute.

"Sure is," he managed to say before eating another forkful of eggs.

I decided to ignore him and went to slip the jersey on

before handing my note to Aunt Coralee. She read it then smiled softly. "Sure, sweetie. That's fine. I expected this."

Relieved, I took my plate of food from her hands and moved to the table.

"What did you expect?" Brady asked.

"That she'd start riding with West to school soon."

Brady smirked again. "So, she's riding with West today?"

I nodded as Aunt Coralee said, "Yes."

Brady was being weird, so I decided to ignore him. I was excited about riding with West. I was excited about his seeing me in a jersey. I was also excited about just seeing him.

He gave me a reason to love life again. I'd not really lived in two years, and I finally realized now I had missed so much. Not speaking had protected me in many ways, but it had also isolated me. From everyone.

When Aunt Coralee walked upstairs, Brady looked over at me. "What I warned you about with West is still something you need to remember. But I admit he is different with you. I've never seen him treat anyone the way he treats you. So maybe this is more to him than other relationships have been. I'm just afraid you could be a crutch to get him through dealing with his dad's death. When someone else he wants comes along, he might take her. You'd be forgotten," he said, then he stood up. "Guard your heart. He won't mean to hurt you. But in the end he might."

A sharp knock interrupted Brady. He glanced at the door as I stood up. I knew it was West. I grabbed my plate and took it to the sink before hurrying to the door.

I opened the door. West smiled the moment our eyes met. Then the smile faltered as he looked down at my jersey. "You're wearing Brady's jersey," he said as his eyes found mine again.

I smiled and nodded. I wanted him to be happy I was showing my support for the team, and for him.

Brady let out a snicker, and I turned to see him covering his mouth as he turned to walk up the stairs. Why was he laughing? Had I done something wrong?

West's arm went around my waist, and he took my book bag with his other hand as he glared after Brady.

"Let's go," he said, sounding less than pleased.

"Did I do something wrong?" I asked, feeling sick to my stomach. West's happy smile was gone.

He didn't reply as he opened his truck door and put my bag in. Then he grabbed me by the waist and lifted me as if I were a child and couldn't get in by myself.

Once I was in the seat, I was at eye level with him. He leaned in and kissed me. It wasn't the sweet, tender kind of kiss I was used to, but it was just as good. I felt like he was marking me and trying to drink me in all at the same time. He had me clinging to him and melting against him by the time he pulled away.

"You can't wear Brady's jersey," he said simply, then closed the door and headed for the driver's side.

If I couldn't wear Brady's jersey, then why was he taking me to school in it?

"I need to change, then," I said as he opened his door and climbed inside.

He nodded in agreement. "Buckle up," he instructed me.

I did as I was told, and he pulled out onto the street and headed for school. I waited for him to explain about the jersey, but he never said anything. At all.

The five-minute drive to Lawton High was short, and I wanted to know why I couldn't wear Brady's jersey. I started to open my mouth, when West drove past the parking lot and toward the field house.

Was he going to make me take it off and leave it in there? Because Aunt Coralee was right; I couldn't wear this tank top to school. I'd be sent home fast.

"What are we doing?" I asked as his door swung open and he got out. He closed it and headed to my side without answering me.

When he opened my door, he grabbed me and kissed me again before picking me up and putting me down on the ground. "We're going to fix your jersey," he said simply. Then took my hand, and we walked inside the field house.

It was deserted this morning, thank goodness. I didn't want to see naked guys. That would be very embarrassing. West took me past a row of lockers, then stopped once he got to the large ones on the end. I saw his last name written above a locker right before he opened it up.

"Take that off," he said as he reached into the locker to pull out a neatly folded jersey on the top shelf.

He was giving me his jersey. My heart rate picked up as I quickly took off Brady's jersey. West turned to look at me and stopped. Instead of handing me the shirt, he stepped toward me and bent his head to kiss my exposed collarbone before burying his head in my neck and inhaling deeply.

I shivered but remained very still. I was afraid if I moved, it would break the spell. I didn't want him to stop. I loved having him close to me like this.

His hand slid around my waist, and he held me against him as his tongue began to take little licks of my neck, followed by kisses. I dropped Brady's jersey and grabbed West's arms to keep my knees from buckling.

"Taste so good, smell so good," he whispered as his mouth moved lower, and he brushed his lips across the tops of my breasts several times. I watched him in fascination.

He lifted his eyes to look at me as he pulled my tank top down a little to continue his trail of kisses. "I need to stop. But I need you to tell me to stop." His voice was deep.

I didn't want him to stop. Getting to class had taken a backseat to this.

"If I tug this down any farther, I'm gonna want more. More than you need to give me in a dirty locker room. I swore to myself the next time I touched you like this, I'd have you somewhere special."

He had robbed me of words. I just stood there holding on to his arms as he cupped one of my breasts through my shirt and kissed the top of the other. Then he growled and closed his eyes tightly before dropping his hands and moving away. I felt cold with him gone. I wanted him back.

"Lift your arms," he said as he picked back up the jersey he'd gotten from his locker.

I did as I was told, and he slipped it over my head. Once he was happy that I had it on properly, he stepped back and looked at me. "Just my jersey, Maggie. No one else's. Ever. I don't want anyone's jersey touching you but mine. Keep this one. Wear it any damn time you want, but don't ever put Brady's on again."

Oh.

Okay.

Oh my.

I nodded and resisted the urge to wrap my arms around the shirt I was now wearing, and cuddle with it. It smelled like West. I was never going to want to wash it.

He grinned. "My girl. My fucking jersey."

Would I Be Her Choice?
CHAPTER 38

WEST

Tonight Maggie sat with my mom at the game. Every chance I got, I looked up at them. Maggie would wave most of the time, but then sometimes I'd catch her talking to my mother. My chest would feel so full, I wondered if it could burst.

After each touchdown I'd glance up to see Maggie standing and cheering with a huge grin on her face, my fucking jersey covering her body. God, I loved that. Everyone saw she was mine.

When I'd seen her in Brady's jersey this morning, I'd wanted to take it off her and burn it. The amused smirk on Brady's face hadn't helped. He'd known when she'd asked

him for it how I'd react. Asswipe had done it on purpose
and gotten a kick out of it.

When he'd walked down the hall and seen her in my
jersey, he'd burst out laughing. No one but the three of us
knew what he found so funny.

Maggie had even grinned and ducked her head as her
cheeks flushed. She had been trying to please me. She just had
no idea that a girl wearing a guy's jersey meant she was his.

Family or not, she wasn't wearing Brady's fucking jersey. Or anyone else's for that matter. Just mine.

We won by a touchdown. Gunner caught a beautiful pass
and ran it in to win us the game in the final three minutes. It
had been a high-scoring game for both teams. I was worried
at one point that we'd need to go into overtime, but Gunner
fixed that.

When I walked out of the locker room, Maggie was
standing there waiting on me. Her smile when our eyes
locked eased the sadness I'd felt when I walked out and my
dad wasn't there.

"You were amazing. . . . I think. I don't know much
about it. But you look really good in those pants," she said
in a whisper when I got close enough to hold her.

Chuckling, I kissed her forehead, then her nose, and
finally her mouth.

"Seeing you up there in my jersey, looking like an angel, helped. I'm gonna need that every game now."

She smiled. "I think I can make that happen."

Tonight I was taking her to the field party. Although she'd been to many, tonight she'd actually attend one. She would be with me. Not hiding in the dark corners waiting for Brady.

The idea of his leaving her out there still pissed me off. I didn't like thinking about how alone she'd been. How no one had been there for her.

"Good game, babe." I looked up from my own private little world with Maggie to see Raleigh standing there.

"Thanks, but I'm not your babe," I replied, trying to get her to leave.

Raleigh laughed and bit her bottom lip like she thought that was sexy. "Maybe not right now, but you're gonna get bored with the mute girl and want some action eventually. I'll be waiting. I was always there for you when you needed me. I want that back, West. I miss us," she said in a low voice that sounded pleading.

I hated it when people took potshots at Maggie. I'd planned to be nice to Raleigh while firmly sending her on her way. But she'd gone and said shit to piss me off.

"I can talk. I just choose who I talk to. So stop trying to upset me. It's not working."

I stood there staring at Maggie as she spoke so clearly and matter-of-factly to Raleigh.

"So you do talk. Huh. Does Brady know this?" Raleigh asked, and I took a step toward her, putting myself between her and Maggie. But Maggie's hand touched my arm as she held on to it and moved to stand beside me.

"Yes, he does. Now you can leave," Maggie said, not backing down.

I stared down at her. Was there nothing about her that wasn't perfect? She even dealt with my ex-girlfriend without being dramatic.

"God, you can't even stop looking at her," Raleigh said in a disgusted tone.

She was right. I couldn't.

I didn't look up, but I knew Raleigh had left once Maggie's shoulders relaxed and she turned to meet my gaze.

"I've decided that I need to enter the world again. Engage. Speak. But until I tell my aunt and uncle, I'm not going to talk to anyone else. Except you, of course."

Except me. I kissed her hard on the lips and tried like hell not to let the fear of losing her take control of me. I wanted her to talk. I wanted her to live her life to the fullest. I just didn't know if I trusted that I'd be enough for her then. Right now I was her world because she spoke only to me. And my mom.

When she talked to other people and let them in . . . would she still choose to be with me?

I had Maggie's hand tucked inside mine as we walked toward the guys at the party. Brady was parking his truck up here again now that he didn't have Maggie hiding out in the dark by herself. Nash was the first one to notice us, and he gave me a tight smile. He still hadn't warmed up to the idea of me and Maggie. But it wasn't because he didn't like her. . . . It was the opposite.

Knowing he'd seen her wearing my jersey all day made the jealous monster inside me stay down. As soon as Nash had met Maggie, he'd recognized something special in her. Same as I had. He'd just not been dealing with shit that made him an idiot. . . .

Lucky for me, she recognized something inside me, too, and overlooked that I was an idiot.

"You ready for this?" I asked her as we got close to the guys.

She tilted her head back to look up at me, and smiled.

That was all I needed.

"Welcome to the family, Maggie," Ryker said, holding up his beer, a big grin on his face. "'Bout time you joined us."

I glanced at Brady. It was his fault she'd not been with us from the beginning. He should feel like shit that he'd left her out there alone. But the look on his face eased my anger some. He wasn't proud of himself, I could see that much.

Ivy was curled up at his side again tonight. I never knew when they were on again or off again. Brady just seemed so detached from her. Like he was letting her stay here because she wanted to. Not because he wanted her here.

"Three games. Three wins. I can taste State already," Asa said as he walked up to the group and took a seat beside Ivy and Brady on the tailgate.

I didn't want to share a seat with anyone. Just Maggie. I led her over to the hay bale that was unoccupied, and sat on it before tugging her down to sit on my lap.

I pressed a kiss to her ear then whispered. "You thirsty? I forgot to get you something."

She shook her head and leaned into me. I held her close, not paying any attention to the others, until I heard Nash say my name. It was hard snapping out of my thoughts about Maggie to respond.

She was just more interesting than he was.

"What?" I asked, turning my attention to Nash.

"You had Tennessee recruiting you. That still a go, or are you holding out for Bama?"

Football. Next year. Something I hadn't thought about. Didn't want to think about. Not with Dad gone. Not with Maggie here.

I shrugged because I didn't know the answer. Yes, Tennessee was watching me. I just didn't care.

"We all got decisions to make. Let's wait until football season is over before we make them. Tonight we need to be talking about Gunner's lightning feet," Brady said, changing the subject and shutting that down.

Gunner held up his beer. "To me. Because I kick ass!" he yelled, and everyone laughed and held up their cups.

Maggie's shoulders shook with silent laughter, and she laid her head on my shoulder as she watched them.

And I watched her.

You're Gonna Own Me
CHAPTER 39

MAGGIE

Listening to West laugh and talk with his friends while he held me in his arms was perfect. It was exactly how I wanted my first real field party experience to be. I couldn't imagine it any other way now.

We didn't stay as long as the others. After an hour or so West was ready to leave. I knew we weren't going home yet, and I was happy to go with him wherever. I argued with him over what was considered good music as we drove up to the bluff. He liked country music of all kinds, but I preferred classic rock.

When he finally parked in our spot, he reached over and turned off the radio before cupping my face in his hands and kissing me like I was something precious. This was my favorite kind of kiss. I loved them all, but when he did this, it made me feel like nothing could touch me. Like nothing could ever hurt me again.

I lost myself in his touch, and it wasn't until he broke our kiss that I opened my eyes and remembered I wasn't floating on a cloud.

"Do you want me with you when you tell your aunt and uncle you're going to talk again?" It was a question, but I heard the hope in his voice. He wanted to be there with me. This was important to him. And that made me love him even more.

"Yes," I replied.

He let out a breath he'd been holding. "Good. I'd be worried about you if I weren't there. I want to be there for you, Maggie. I don't . . ." He stopped and glanced off toward the town's lights below us. "I don't want you to feel like you always have to be my strength. I want to be that for you, too." He shifted his gaze back to me. "I want to mean to you what you mean to me."

That wasn't an "I love you," but it was close enough. That last sentence said more than he knew. I could tell he was worried that he wouldn't be as important to me once I started talking to other people. He didn't want to lose the connection we had.

I reached up and cupped his face this time. "Before you, I never smiled. I never laughed. I'd forgotten how. I was alone, and I didn't know any other way. But you saved me. You make me feel appreciated, needed, wanted. You brought me out, and you gave me reasons to laugh again. Just seeing you makes me smile. No one could ever mean to me what you mean to me."

West grinned like a little boy who had been given his ultimate wish, and then he held me against him so tightly, I could hardly breathe. I didn't complain, but when he eased up, I took a deep breath.

He stared down at me for a few moments before his hand slid between my thighs. "How are you . . . there?" he asked, holding his hand close enough to make tingles start between my legs but not so close as to actually brush against me.

"Not sore anymore," I replied, feeling my face get hot.

He inhaled sharply, and his nostrils flared. The heat in his eyes was enough to turn on all my switches. "I don't want you to think that this . . . that this is . . . what we are about. I've had that kind of relationship, and it's empty. And it's not us. What we have is more. I want you to always know you're more. So, if you want to stop and not do that again . . . I'll understand. I'm okay even if I just get to hold you."

He was worried I'd think he just wanted sex. He was

wrapping himself so tightly around my heart, I feared it was too much. Too fast. But I wouldn't stop it.

"I want us to be more," I replied. "But I like that, too."

West let out a soft chuckle. "You're gonna own me."

I reached down and took his hand and slid it up to where I wanted it to be. "I want more of this with you."

West's strong fingers moved my shorts out of the way and were inside without any more argument. I arched my back and cried out from the sudden pleasure. He held on to me as he kissed down my neck, telling me how perfect, beautiful, and special I was. He never said I love you, but neither did I.

Hours later I was tucked into bed, when West climbed in through my window. I opened my eyes and watched as he slipped off his boots and jeans then climbed in with me. Once he had me curled up on his chest, he kissed the top of my head. "One day I'm going to make love to you on a bed," he whispered.

I drifted off to sleep, thinking about West and I doing something much more interesting than just sleeping in my bed.

When I woke the next morning, West was gone, and the sun was pouring in through my windows. I buried my head in the pillow he'd been sleeping on and inhaled deeply. I loved smelling him.

I got up and went to get dressed so I could go down and eat breakfast. Also, I wanted to let Aunt Corlaee know that I'd like to talk to her, Uncle Boone, and Brady sometime today. Whenever she said was a good time, I'd let West know.

Today was a big day for me. Today I would stop hiding. I'd make real relationships with my family. I was excited about that. But I was also scared. Afraid of what they'd ask me. Terrified they'd want me to speak of that day. I didn't want to describe that day again. Ever.

Having West beside me while I told them would help, and it would explain a lot about my relationship with him that I knew they didn't understand. But I needed them to be clear that I wouldn't talk about that day to them or anyone else. I never wanted to mention my father again. If they wanted to talk about my mother and fond memories of her, I could do that. I wanted that now.

I was ready for that now.

Brady was sitting at the table, his hair sticking up in random places, wearing only a pair of plaid pajama pants while he ate a bowl of cereal and drank a cup of coffee. The newspaper was open to the sports section, and he was reading it intently.

Aunt Coralee was standing at the bar in the kitchen, writing down a list. It was for groceries. I knew that list. She did it every Saturday. She looked up at me when I entered, and beamed a bright, cheery smile.

"Good morning. I'm ashamed to say I didn't cook any breakfast. We're out of most everything. I'm going to run to the store this afternoon and get what we need. But for now you'll have to make due with cereal or toast. I think we have some fresh fruit, too."

I was good with a bowl of cereal. It was what I'd lived off of during my two years with Jorie. She hadn't cooked at all. But she'd also rarely been home. I'd lived alone for the most part.

Brady glanced up at me then went back to reading his paper and eating.

I walked over to Aunt Coralee and laid down the note I'd written about talking to them today. I figured walking down here and announcing we needed to discuss the fact I was talking again would be too much of a surprise. I also wouldn't get a chance to tell them what I was willing to talk about and what I wasn't.

I didn't want to go to a counselor, therapist, shrink— whatever you call them. I'd been to ten of those. None of them had helped me at all. I wasn't going back, and they needed to know that.

Aunt Coralee read the note then looked up at me with a concerned frown. "Sure, sweetheart. We can talk now if you like," she said.

Brady jerked his head up and looked back at us. "Talk about what?" he asked.

"Maggie wants to talk to all of us about something," she said, glancing at him for a moment before looking back at me. "Here, you can use my pen." She handed me her pen.

I shook my head. Then I pointed to the part in the note that said all three of them.

Her frown deepened. "Okay. Yes. Well, let me go get your uncle Boone. He's outside, cutting grass."

She patted my arm and hurried for the door. She wasn't going to give me much time to get West here. I didn't try texting him in case he was asleep. I called instead.

He answered on the first ring.

She's Just Like Her Momma

CHAPTER 40

WEST

Maggie was waiting outside on the porch swing when I pulled up. She'd called me just as I was getting out of the shower. Somehow I'd made it here in ten minutes. My hair had still been wet and I hadn't been able to find any underwear, but I'd made it.

She stood up from the swing and walked over to the top of the steps. "Hey," I said, pressing a kiss to her lips. "You ready to do this?"

I could see the anxiety in her eyes when she nodded. I slipped my hand over hers. This time I would be the one holding her up. She'd make it through this. I wouldn't let go.

"They're waiting. Brady heard me call you, so he

explained that I was waiting on you and I wanted you in on this conversation. But I think I've worried them. Brady knows, but Aunt Coralee and Uncle Boone look really concerned."

I tilted my head toward the door. "Let's go do this, then. I'll be right there the whole time."

She gave me a relieved smile, and my heart thudded against my chest. She made me feel things I'd never felt before. Things I wanted more of. Things I didn't want to live without.

I followed her inside and, sure enough, all three Higgenses were sitting in the living room, waiting. Brady was the only one who was relaxed and looked bored. His parents were on the edges of their seats. There was a note pad and a pencil on the table in front of Coralee. I wondered if she'd brought that for this discussion.

Maggie walked to stand in front of them all, and I squeezed her hand. She could do this. I'd make sure she could.

"I want to talk again," she said in a soft voice that startled both her aunt and uncle. I'd never seen Boone's eyes get so wide.

"I want to be a part of this family. I'm ready for that. But I need you to understand something," she said to them, then glanced at me. Her hand was still tucked inside mine, and I nodded to reassure her. "I don't want to talk about . . . that day. I don't want to talk about him. I don't want to talk to a therapist. I do want to talk about my mom. Good memories. I like thinking about her, and I've talked about her with West a lot. He listens, but I'd like to share memories with other people who knew her and loved her. But the rest . . . I can't. I stopped talking to protect myself. From me and from everyone else. It's how I survived." She stopped and waited.

Coralee stood and tears welled up in her eyes. "We won't make you talk about anything you don't want to, Maggie. I promise you that. I'm just—" She let out a small sob. "It's good to hear your voice again," she finally said before covering her mouth and letting out another sob.

Maggie's shoulders eased some. That was what she'd needed to hear.

Boone looked at me then back at Maggie. "I reckon he's who got you to talk. He needed you, and you knew you could help him, so you talked. Sounds like something your momma would have done." He moved his attention back to me. "She's just like her momma. Special, kind, sweet. But strong, too. She's survived a lot. And if this," he said, pointing at the two of us, "is more than friendship now, then you be sure you're ready to cherish her. You hurt her, and I'll hurt you. Don't care who you are."

He was protecting her. Like a father. Like her father

should be doing. I'd always liked Boone Higgens, but he'd just climbed a notch in my eyes. He was being the father Maggie needed. The one she'd been given had destroyed her life. Now Boone was going to protect it.

I nodded. "Yes, sir. I know how special she is. I would never hurt her. I swear."

He didn't seem convinced, but he looked back at Maggie. "I love you, little girl. I loved your momma. Losing her changed all our lives, but it especially changed yours. We want to help you heal. If you'll let us."

A tear rolled down Maggie's face, and I had to fight my instinct to grab her and comfort her. She needed this with them. I couldn't step in now.

"Thank you. I . . . like it here. I like this house and all of you. I feel safe, and it's been a long time since I've felt safe. Thank you for giving me a home."

Brady stood up. "I'm just glad you came so I could finally get my attic bedroom," he said, then winked at her.

Maggie laughed, and I fought the little bit of jealousy that tugged at me over someone else making her laugh. I loved her laugh, but it seemed I was getting possessive of it.

She had a family now. One she would allow into her world.

Maggie wouldn't be silent anymore.

*　　*　　*

I left Maggie with her aunt Coralee to go grocery shopping after lunch. I needed to get home, because my momma wanted me there to tell my grandmother good-bye today. I had managed to dodge the woman most of the time she'd been there. The only time Momma hadn't been with her was at my game last night.

Walking inside I stopped when I saw several suitcases by the front door. One of those being my mother's. My grandmother was sitting on the sofa, her back straight and her hands in her lap as if she were posing for a photo. It was creepy as hell.

"Momma?" I called out instead of speaking to that woman.

My mother came around the corner, another duffel bag on her arm. She looked nervous and uncertain. My stomach knotted up. I wasn't moving. We hadn't talked about this yet, but I sure as hell wasn't leaving Lawton.

"What's going on?" I asked, afraid to step any farther into the room.

Momma gave me a sad look, then put the bag down on top of her suitcase. "I wanted to talk to you about this before you left this morning, but you just took off. Which is okay. You have a life. I don't want your life to change. I just . . ." She glanced at her mother then back at me. "I need a break from here. Being in this house is hard on me.

I keep thinking your dad is going to walk in the door any minute. I miss him, and being here makes that so much worse. I just need a break. I would love for you to go with me, but I know with football and Maggie . . . I don't expect you to. I won't be gone but a couple of weeks. Please understand. I can't be here all day alone with his memory." Her eyes filled with tears and began to roll down her face.

"You want to go to Louisiana?" I'd been there, and I couldn't understand why anyone would choose to visit my grandmother's house. It wouldn't be an uplifting trip. She'd be in hell with that woman and in that house.

She nodded and wiped at her face. "It was my home once. I know you don't have fond memories of it, but I do. I need something to take my mind off the pain. The sadness."

This was her choice to make, and I wanted her to be happy again. I hated thinking of her in pain and suffering here alone while I went to school and practice and spent time with Maggie. And I would miss her, but I wasn't leaving Lawton.

"You're eighteen. You're a man now. You'll be fine here while I'm gone. You have your friends and Maggie. The moment you need me, call me and I'll be here. But I have to get away, West. I have to."

I did the only thing I could do. I walked over and hugged her. We had both lost Dad. I'd had Maggie to help me deal with the pain. She had no one. "I love you, Momma. I understand."

She sniffed and squeezed me tightly around the waist. "I love you too, and I'm so proud of you."

But she was leaving me. Dad had just left us, and she was leaving me too.

She's Been Paying Attention
in Her Silent Wonderland
CHAPTER 41

MAGGIE

Shopping for groceries with Aunt Coralee was interesting. She chatted a lot and asked all kinds of questions. I didn't realize how much she hadn't found out about me yet. I enjoyed it more than I thought I would.

When we got home, Brady was outside playing basketball with Asa, Gunner, Ryker, and Nash. Aunt Coralee stopped and tossed them all Gatorades from one of the bags before she went on inside. They each grabbed a couple of bags too, and the car was quickly unloaded.

I helped her put things away and had just started heading up to my room when Gunner stopped me. "Hey, you gonna talk to us now too?"

I hadn't told Brady not to say anything to his friends. They were West's friends too. But now that they knew I was speaking, I wasn't sure how to handle them. I didn't want a million questions from them, either.

"It's okay. He told us you got limits. Come on and hang out down here with us," Ryker called out as he sank onto the sofa, a bag of chips in his hand.

I turned around and walked back down the steps. If I wanted to fit into West's world, I would have to do this.

"You've been whispering to West for weeks. I've seen it," Nash said from his perch on the barstool. "I tried to get you to talk to me, but nothing. West crooks his finger, and you start chatting him up."

"Nash." Brady's tone held a warning.

Nash shrugged, then smirked at me. "It's okay. You can come talk to me now."

"I asked her to stay down here and talk to us. She can come talk to me," Ryker argued.

I glanced at Brady, who shrugged and rolled his eyes before grabbing the Xbox remote and sitting down on a beanbag chair.

Gunner's arm rested on my shoulders, startling me. "She wants to talk to me, dontcha, sugar?" he said, sounding like his usual cocky, arrogant self.

"Gonna get that arm ripped off if West shows up," Asa warned him.

Gunner flexed his arm that was around my shoulders. "I ain't scared of West. He won't hurt these priceless receiving arms."

"Shi-it," Asa drawled, shaking his head and picking up the other Xbox remote.

"Y'all, back off her. She decided she wants to talk, and y'all are gonna have her changing her mind," Brady grumbled without taking his eyes off the screen.

"I just want to hear her say something," Nash called from across the room.

I could stand here silent and let them go on and on, or I could say something and get this awkward moment behind me. Sucking in the courage I needed, I turned to Nash. "What would you like me to say?" I asked.

The room went silent. Then Nash's face broke into a grin. "Well, hell, Maggie. Even your voice is pretty."

"I was thinking the same thing," Gunner added, still draped around me.

"Thank you," I replied, not really knowing what to say to that.

"You're welcome, sugar," Gunner said, sounding amused.

"Seriously, get your arm off her before West gets here," Nash said, glaring at Gunner.

"You ain't worried about West. You're just jealous. You've been after her since she showed up. But you moved too slow and, dude, you snooze, you lose," Gunner taunted him. I decided to end this before it got ridiculous.

I moved away from Gunner, causing him to drop his arm.

"I'm not your sugar," I informed him. "And, seriously, if a girl likes being your 'sugar,' she needs her head evaluated."

"And that's how you burn his ass," Ryker said through his laughter.

"Everyone knows that Gunner loves Gunner more than anyone else. A girl would be naïve to think differently," I added.

Gunner laughed this time. "She's been paying attention in her silent wonderland."

"That ain't real hard to figure out, douche," Asa said with a chuckle.

"Not to change the subject, but did y'all know Riley Young was back in town?" Nash asked, looking from Brady to Gunner almost nervously.

Gunner's easygoing demeanor died. Coldness came over his face that I'd never seen before. "She won't stay long. No one wants her here," he said as he stalked back toward the kitchen.

Once he was out of the room, Brady stopped playing long enough to shoot an annoyed look at Nash. "Did you have to bring that shit up? We all knew she was back. No reason to point it out. I saw her at a field party a couple of weeks back. I made sure she knew she wasn't wanted, and then I told him I'd seen her."

"You saw her at a party? Fuck. She's got nerve," Asa said, sounding amazed.

"She didn't stay. Never saw her come into the clearing. Doubt she got out of her car."

The dark-haired girl who'd driven up that night and who Brady had glared at before walking off. I'd forgotten about that. That had to be who they were talking about. But why did they hate her?

"Riley Young don't belong here. We'll all make sure she gets that message if she tries coming back to Lawton High. No one wants her there. And Gunner doesn't need that screwing with his head," Brady said as if he could control it all.

She had been beautiful. I remembered that much. And she'd seemed sad and lonely. I couldn't imagine that the girl I'd seen that night had done something so horrible, they all had a reason to hate her. Especially Gunner.

There was a knock at the front door before it swung open. West walked in, and his eyes immediately locked on me. I forgot everything else, and smiled. He made me smile. I couldn't help it.

I Can't Be Your Crutch
CHAPTER 42

WEST

The weekend went fast. Too Fast. I wasn't home enough to notice Momma wasn't there. But then I also wasn't going home, because it was too hard. I slept in Maggie's room until five then snuck out and went to my house to shower, change, and eat before heading out again. I just couldn't stay there long.

It was the laughter that haunted me most. The times I'd run in the house, excited about something and Dad and Mom were there to listen to me. Our family dinners always came back to me as I sat at the table and ate all alone.

Monday morning, though, I was focused on Maggie. She'd be going to school today without her safety walls of silence in place. Her aunt was going with her this morning to talk to the principal about Maggie's decision to speak. Also about Maggie's preference not to have to see a counselor.

I wanted to pick her up and take her, but I settled for waiting outside the office until Maggie and Coralee walked out. The late bell hadn't rung yet, but I wasn't concerned with being late. I was worried about Maggie. She was going to have to face first period without me. Hell, she had to face all her periods without me.

Maggie's eyes lit up when she saw me standing there, and she immediately came over to me and slipped her hand in mine. "Good morning," I said, loving that she came to me so easily.

"Good morning," she replied, then glanced back at her aunt. "I'll see you after school."

"Y'all, have a good day," Coralee called after us as we walked off toward our lockers.

"Didn't like not taking you to school today," I said as soon as we were far enough away from Coralee.

"I missed you too," she replied, a smirk on her sweet lips.

"Wish I were going with you to all your classes."

She squeezed my hand. "I'll be okay. Promise."

I knew she would, but that didn't change the fact I wanted to be holding her hand. I wanted to be there, making sure everyone was nice to her. That no one was too nice to her and that . . . No. I had to get control of myself. I didn't want to smother her with my possessiveness. She was learning to live again, and I had to let her breathe.

It wasn't until after third period that the fact she was talking to other people really hit home for me.

Seeing Vance Young standing at her locker as she looked up at him and talked to him felt like a fucking slice in my gut. I hated that. She was mine. She talked only to me. I didn't want to share her.

My dad was gone. My mother had left me. And I wouldn't lose Maggie.

"Back off, Young," I snarled as I shoved him away from Maggie and slid my arm around her waist, pulling her against me.

"What the fuck, West?" Vance said, glaring at me. "You mad because my sister's back? Y'all are a bunch of fuckers, you know that? You don't know shit about what happened. About her."

This wasn't about Riley. That was Gunner's battle, not mine.

"I couldn't give a shit if Riley's back in town or not. But don't get that close to my girl again."

Vance looked down at Maggie then back at me. "I thought y'all were friends. That's what Serena said last period. I didn't know she was yours."

"She's mine," I said, leaving no room for doubt.

Vance shrugged and held up his hands. "Sorry. Thought she was single."

After he left, I looked down at Maggie. She was standing very still and staring vacantly at the wall across from us. "Hey, what's wrong?"

She didn't reply at first, and I was worried she was having some sort of panic attack because she'd started talking to everyone. But finally she turned and looked up at me. "You're going to have to let people talk to me, West."

Yeah, I knew that.

"You can't shove them away and claim that I'm yours. It doesn't work that way."

Wait . . . what? "If another guy is hitting on you, then I sure as hell can. He needed to know you were taken."

She frowned and tilted her head. Dark hair fell over one shoulder. "Will you act this way when every guy talks to me?"

Probably. Yes. I shrugged.

She let out a sigh, and her shoulders fell. "What are we, West? Because I'm not sure. You say I'm yours, but what does that mean?"

Was she kidding? I thought I had made that very clear a few hundred times already.

"You're it for me, Maggie. I don't ever want anyone else."

She gave me a sad smile, then reached up to touch my face. "But if you're going to be upset every time a guy talks to me, you'll be miserable. Isn't it enough for me to be your girlfriend and to trust me? I'd never do anything to hurt you."

"I do trust you, and you're so much more than my girlfriend. But I just need to protect you."

She let out a small laugh. "From the world? Because you can't."

She didn't get it. She was all I had left. She was the only person I loved who hadn't left me.

"Yes, I can," I replied, my tone harsher than I'd intended.

Maggie frowned, and I saw disappointment flash in her eyes. I didn't want that. I'd seen her look at me like that before, and I hated it. I never wanted to let her down. I just needed her to accept I wasn't sharing. I couldn't. I needed her.

"West, this . . . thing we have. It's—" She closed her eyes and took a deep breath. "I was there for you when you needed someone. And maybe I've become more of a crutch for you. You get angry if anyone gets near me or speaks to me, and that's not normal. It's unhealthy. I've never given you a reason to be so possessive. This thing between us can't work if you hover over me like a madman."

What the hell did that mean? I just wanted to keep her safe. How was that making me unhealthy? We weren't messed up. And, yes, I was jealous, but that was normal. It was normal for me to be jealous. I was in love with her. "I can't lose you. I can't survive. . . ." I paused. "I need you to make it."

Maggie let out a heavy sigh as she took a step back from me. I fought the urge to reach out and grab her and pull her close again. The distance terrified me.

"That's not what a relationship is. You have the strength inside of you to survive. You don't need me to do that." She paused and closed her eyes tightly as if she were fighting back tears. I started to reach for her and apologize. Anything to make the sadness on her face go away. But she opened her eyes and stared up at me with a determination that still held unshed tears. "I think it's best if we take a step back. I wanted to be the shoulder you could lean on and the one you could talk to. I wanted you to have everything I didn't. But now I see it's made us something that will never work. I can't be your crutch. That's not fair to either of us." She reached up and wiped away the single tear that had slid down her face, then stepped back from me some more. "I didn't mean for this to happen. I never meant . . ." She trailed off and covered her mouth as a sob broke free. "I can't do this, West."

I heard her words, but my mind was screaming for her to stop. She couldn't be saying what it sounded like. But before I could say anything, she turned and walked away. Leaving me alone. Again.

Then she turned and ran. She didn't look back.

I stood, helpless and unable to react. The emptiness that haunted me before was clawing at my chest to get back in and suck the life from me. But more than that . . . I was lost and broken.

The one person I thought I could trust had just let me down.

He Wasn't Alone. I Was.

CHAPTER 43

MAGGIE

Sitting in my room alone was all I wanted to do. Facing how unhealthy my relationship with West had become wasn't easy. It was even harder to push him away. Which didn't say much for me. The fact was, I still wanted him. He wasn't the only one guilty here. I was too. I'd created this. I had let him become dependent on me.

This wasn't what I'd intended to happen in the beginning. I had imagined finding a way for me to heal too while I helped him. It was a way for me to find peace. But we had become something more. Something I never imagined. Falling in love with West Ashby had not been part of my plan.

Having to face the truth and let him go was a result of that stupid emotion I'd fallen victim to. Love. But West didn't love me in return. He needed me only to get through. One day he wouldn't need me anymore, and that would be it. There would be no foundation there for us except a shared pain from losing a parent.

A swift knock on the door was followed by Brady's entrance before I could invite even him inside. The frown etched on his forehead told me he knew. West had said something to him. I wished he hadn't. I didn't want to talk about it yet.

"Are you okay?" he asked, studying me closely.

I wanted to tell him yes so he would leave, his duties as caring cousin fulfilled. But the words wouldn't come. I shrugged instead.

Brady nodded as if that made complete sense. "He's not okay either. Don't guess you want to tell me about it?"

No, I didn't. Verbalizing it made it real. Just thinking about it in my head was easier.

"He's attached to you. I've never seen him act about anyone the way he does about you. Honestly, it concerned me. You've been through too much to be expected to take on his baggage too. He needs to realize he can survive this without you holding him up."

That made it sound like I'd abandoned West. I didn't

like thinking about it that way. I'd never do that. "He got furious because another guy talked to me today," I replied. "It's not . . . healthy. He looks at me like I am his possession to protect so no one can snatch me away. We're only in high school. That's not normal."

Brady walked over and sat on the edge of my bed. "I agree. It's not. But West has always had a temper. Even when we were kids. I think a bit of that is coming through now. Not that it makes it okay. It doesn't. You're a person. Not his personal belonging."

"Exactly," I muttered, feeling guilty for talking about him like this. He wasn't here to defend himself, and I was telling his best friend things I shouldn't.

"He wanted to come over. I told him no. That he needs to give you time to work through whatever you're dealing with," Brady explained. "You did the right thing."

But West was alone. He had no one there with him. "He's all by himself," I said, feeling the guilt weigh heavily on my already aching heart.

Brady stood up. "I'm headed over there now. I called Nash already, and he should be there any minute. We got him. You take care of you. This past month you've made breakthroughs no one thought you could. You're talking, Maggie. That means you're healing. Focus on you. I'll take care of West."

My eyes stung from unshed tears as I nodded. He was right. West had someone. In fact he had a whole group of friends who would stand with him through anything. He wasn't alone.

I was.

When I finally fell asleep last night, Brady still hadn't returned. I was relieved. Knowing he was staying with West had helped me calm down enough to sleep. Today I'd have to face school. I'd have to face West. I'd have to face my choice.

Getting up was harder than going to sleep had been. I wanted to stay hidden away in my room for weeks. Until my chest didn't hurt anymore. I had known from the start that West Ashby could hurt me if I let him in. I just hadn't expected it to feel like this. I had imagined him breaking it off with me because he wanted someone else. Or he was bored.

This was so much harder. I had been the one to hurt him. Me. The look on his face wouldn't stop taunting me. Reminding me of how much it had crushed me to say those words to him.

"Hungry? I made waffles," Aunt Coralee said as I walked into the kitchen. Eating made me feel nauseous, but she'd made a stack of waffles, and I knew Brady wasn't here to eat them.

"Brady isn't here," I said, hoping she knew that already. I didn't want to get him in trouble.

She gave me a sad smile and nodded. "I know. I'm about to take these over to West's. There's a houseful of boys who need food. I spoke with Brady thirty minutes ago." She walked over to me, put her arm around my shoulders, and then kissed the top of my head. "Are you okay?" she asked softly.

I nodded simply because I didn't want to talk about it.

She squeezed me to her. "In life we often have to make decisions that aren't easy. But it doesn't mean they aren't right."

"But what if they're wrong?" I asked before I could stop myself.

She let me go and moved to fix me a plate. "Then fate steps in and fixes things. You just have to trust it."

I didn't say any more. But her words played over in my head, and I hoped she was right.

You'll Lose Her If You Don't
CHAPTER 44

WEST

"Mom's bringing waffles," Brady said as he opened the curtains in my room and let the sunlight pour inside. "Get up and get showered. Nash is still asleep on the sofa. I'll throw some ice on him before I leave. It's the only way he'll get up."

We had stayed up most of the night. The guys had tried to get my mind off things, but it hadn't worked. They just made it so I hadn't been alone. If I had, I'd have ended up at Maggie's window. More than once last night I wondered if that was why Brady had come over with all the guys. To keep me from going to Maggie. I wanted to resent him for it, but he was the only one who could keep me sane right now.

He told me about talking to her and how he really felt like she needed time to herself, to accept how far she'd come. It was all too much for her, and I was scaring her with my intensity on top of it. Thing was, I didn't know how to be any other way with her. She made me a little crazy.

"You taking Maggie to school?" I asked him, knowing the answer.

He didn't say anything at first, but finally he gave me one small nod. "I'll eat at my house. The rest of the guys are up and dressed, waiting on Mom to come feed them. I think they left you hot water."

"How do I handle today?" I asked him before he could leave the room.

He turned to glance back at me. "You give her space. You realize you can survive without her to lean on, and you make it through."

He didn't get it. He'd never been in love. What did he mean by space? Was I just supposed to ignore her? So I asked him, "How do I give her space?"

He shrugged. "You know, just leave her alone. Let her breathe."

"Ignore her?" I asked. My voice was hard and angry, but I couldn't help it.

He raised his eyebrows. "Yeah. I guess so."

I stood up and threw my pillow across the room. "Fuck

that! How the hell am I supposed to ignore her, Brady? Huh? I can't ignore her. I'm in love with her."

I'd never said that aloud before. Not even to her.

"If that's so, then you need to find a way to back off. You'll lose her if you don't."

"I've already lost her." The words sliced through me as I said them.

"No, you haven't. I've talked to her. Remember? I know what she's thinking. All you did was scare her. She believes she's just your crutch and nothing more. That's why she's doing this. I can assure you, she has no idea you love her."

I should have told her. "If I tell her—"

"She won't believe you. She'll think you're telling her whatever it takes to get her back. You're going to have to let her go."

I'd never be able to let her go. But I could pretend that I had if it's what she needed from me. She'd been there for me when I needed her. It was time I did whatever I had to do to make her happy. If stepping back was it, then I'd do it.

Asa and Gunner both stayed until I left the house, trying to get me to ride with one of them. But I wanted the freedom of having my truck. When I finally pulled out of the drive and headed to school, they followed behind me. It was like they had to be sure I was going to show up for class.

I timed it so I was walking in just as the last bell rang. Now we would all be late to first period. But I hadn't asked them to wait on me. I just couldn't handle going to my locker and seeing Maggie. I wouldn't be able to ignore her, and I didn't trust I wouldn't start begging her right there in front of everyone.

"I got Mr. Tremble first period," Asa said with a grin. "He won't count me late," he added as he ran past me.

Gunner came up beside me. "We won't get counted late either if we hurry."

I didn't mind getting a late slip in exchange for putting off going to class. But I knew Coach would have me running suicides after practice if he got word I was late. That was protocol for a player being late to school.

"I need to grab my notebook," I told Gunner.

He shoved a notebook at me. "Use this one and run," he said before breaking into a run himself.

I followed behind him. When practice was over, I wanted to go home and be alone. Last night I hadn't been given room to think. They had all meant well, but being by myself was what I wanted right now.

Gunner opened the door to our first-period class and stepped inside. Mrs. Sentle glanced up at us and frowned, then motioned for us to take a seat. "Glad you could join us, boys" was all she said.

I sat down beside Gunner, who found an empty desk first. He glanced at me and smirked. "Told ya."

"Hey, West," a blonde I didn't know said as she turned to smile at me.

Gunner chuckled beside me. "The news you're a free agent again is out."

I ignored them both. If I was to prove to Maggie that I loved her, then girls like this one weren't going to help. I shot Gunner an annoyed glare.

He just laughed harder. Asshole.

CHAPTER 45

MAGGIE

This was something I had to face sooner or later. I couldn't avoid West. That wasn't possible or fair. Not going to my locker for the first three periods had been tough. It was time I faced reality. Although, he wouldn't actually be there this time because of his schedule, so I wasn't really facing anything yet.

Moving through the crowd, I could feel people watching me. It had been that way all morning. Several girls had called me a bitch and a whore. The general consensus was that I was a horrible person for breaking up with West just after he lost his father. Part of me agreed with them.

When I finally reached my locker, I opened it quickly only

to have it slammed closed by a hand with long red fingernails. The metal door just barely missed my hand as I jerked it back. "You are low-life scum," a female voice hissed in my ear. I knew that voice. I had expected her to confront me at some point today. I just hadn't expected her to do it like this.

I turned to face Raleigh. She was glaring at me with something close to triumph.

"You're a coldhearted bitch," she said loud enough for everyone around us to hear. People got quiet, and I knew we had an audience. That was just going to make her worse.

I didn't respond to her. She was angry because she cared about West. She wanted to be furious with me and to have a right to be. This was her chance.

"Nothing to say? What? You're gonna be silent again?" she asked, then shoved me in the chest until I fell back against the locker behind me.

She pointed her finger in my face, and I wondered if she planned on clawing me with it next. "You weren't good enough for him. You're a freak. Just. A. Freak."

Right before her pointy nail touched my face, she was jerked back.

"Why don't you go take your crazy bitch demonstration somewhere else?" Nash said, moving her away from me and putting himself between us. "I think Maggie has seen enough to know that you are indeed fucked-up."

"You're taking up for her? You're his friend!" Raleigh yelled.

"I'm one of his best friends. And even if Maggie wasn't one of my friends too, I'd be doing this for him. Because West would lose his shit if he'd seen this. Attacking her ain't getting him back, Ray."

"She used him!" Raleigh's voice carried down the hallway now that everyone had gone silent to watch.

"No, Raleigh. She saved him. When no one else could. Now take yourself far away from her before this bat-crazy episode you just had gets back to him. Because he'll come for Maggie first to check on her. Then he's coming for you."

"You're wrong. He'll need me," she said, sounding convinced.

I hated that the idea of West with her or any girl made my stomach twist in knots. I had been the one to end what we had. He would move on. And when he did, I would have to deal with it.

Nash shook his head, then turned back around to face me. The concern in his eyes almost made me cry. I hated drawing attention to myself, but today it seemed like just breathing brought attention I didn't want.

"You good? Bitch is loony as hell," Nash said with a roll of his eyes.

I managed a nod. I wasn't good. But that wasn't Raleigh's fault.

"You look pale," he said, frowning.

"I don't like attention," I whispered, afraid people were still listening to us.

He sighed. "Well, babe, you are going to have to deal with it for a while. I've heard what they're all saying. That's why I came to find you. See if you were okay."

"Thanks," I said through the lump in my throat.

"Get your things. I'm walking you to your next class. I'll have Brady know you need an escort after this one. Between us, we should be able to keep you covered for a while. At least until they find something else to focus on."

I wanted to tell him that I didn't need that. That I could take care of myself. But I couldn't. Because if he hadn't shown up, Raleigh would still be in my face, yelling at me while everyone watched.

"Okay," I replied, and turned back to my locker.

"He's going to be furious when he finds out about this. When he comes to find you, know his anger isn't at you. It's because he thinks he's caused this to happen to you. He wants to protect you. He's not going to take this well."

A tear escaped, and I reached up and wiped it away quickly. If only his need to protect me was something more. Something deeper. Not simply his need to have me beside him so he could cope with things. I wanted to be more to him than someone to lean on.

"Ready," I said as I tucked my books close and fell into step beside Nash.

He didn't ask me questions or mention West. We walked in silence to my next class. Once we were there, I thanked him and went inside. Eyes locked on me, so I dropped my gaze to the books in my arms and found a desk in the back. If I were going to make it through class, I needed to be where as few people as possible could look at me.

I Want to Belong to You

CHAPTER 46

WEST

Nash walked into class just as the late bell rang. His eyes scanned the room until they found me. His frown deepened as he made his way back to where I was sitting. There wasn't an empty seat beside me, but he stopped by a guy with curly hair and glasses and convinced him to move over before taking his seat.

I glanced at him, and he turned his attention to me. "There was a . . . problem at the lockers . . . but I handled it, and she's fine," Nash whispered.

My chest tightened, and I clenched my fists. "Explain," I said, not giving a shit if anyone heard me. I was ready to bolt and go find Maggie. The fact that I was supposed to be giving her room was the only thing keeping me in my seat.

"Raleigh cornered her at her locker."

I didn't need to hear any more. I stood up and started walking for the door.

"Where do you think you're going, Mr. Ashby?" the teacher asked.

"I'm sick," I replied before opening the door and stalking out. I should have found out more from Nash. Like if Raleigh had touched her. But my instinct to go find Maggie and check on her was stronger.

I started toward Maggie's class when the door reopened behind me.

"West, wait," Nash called out.

"Going to find Maggie," I replied, not stopping.

"She's fine. I took care of it," was his response.

"Did Raleigh touch her?" I asked, my voice rising with the thought of anyone hurting Maggie.

Nash didn't respond, and I knew I had my answer.

"She was taking up for you in her crazy-ass way. The females in this school have come to the conclusion Maggie is the enemy, since she broke up with you. Surely, you've heard the talk today. It was bound to happen. Someone was going to confront her."

That made me stop. "What?" I asked him incredulously.

"What do you mean 'what?'?" He looked confused.

"What are they saying?"

"The girls?"

I nodded.

"Shit about Maggie. She's not responding to it; she's keeping her head down. I walked her to class and texted Brady to get her after and walk her to lunch. The buzz will die down soon enough."

"Wait." I stopped him as my stomach twisted and anger pulsed through my veins. "Are you saying that people have been talking shit to Maggie all day about this? Because of me?"

Nash nodded.

"Motherfucker!" I roared, and broke into a run toward Maggie's class.

"I thought you'd have heard them!" Nash called out.

If I had heard them, I would have shut them down. What did he think I was doing? Letting them talk about Maggie? Seriously? Did my own friends not even realize I was in love with her?

I stopped at the door to the classroom she was in and took a deep breath. My emotions were all over the place. I hadn't meant to cause her any pain, yet that was all I seemed to be able to do. She had run from me because I'd acted like an ass. I was clinging to her and not even taking into consideration the fact she had her own demons to face. She needed me, and all I had done was take from her.

I was ready to be her shoulder to cry on. I wanted her to lean on me for a change. I wanted more.

Jerking the door open, I searched the room until I found her in the back, looking like she was ready to crawl under her desk.

"Can I help you, West?" Mr. Banks asked.

"I need to see Maggie, please, sir," I replied, tearing my eyes from her to look at him.

"Uh, well, um . . . okay. But please be quick," he replied.

I turned my gaze back to her. If I could plead with a look, I was doing it. Slowly, she stood up and made her way toward me. Her eyes were on the floor, and her hands were fisted together in front of her. She was nervous. I never wanted to make her nervous.

When she reached me, I stepped back and let her walk out into the hallway before closing the door and giving us the privacy we needed.

"Are you okay?" I asked, fighting the urge to reach out and pull her against me.

"I'm fine," she replied in a whisper.

"I'll handle Raleigh. She won't bother you again. I swear it," I said fiercely.

She shrugged. "She cares about you. She was defending you."

No. Raleigh cared about herself. This hadn't been about me. She'd seen an opening to attack Maggie, and she'd taken it. "If she cared about me, she wouldn't have touched you. People who care about me would protect you. Like Nash."

Maggie lifted her gaze to meet mine. Her eyes reflected so many of the same emotions I was trying to deal with. "I didn't want to hurt you."

"I know. But I was hurting you. I wasn't being what you needed."

She broke our eye contact as she glanced down the hallway. "You just lost your dad, West. I should have been more sensitive."

Screw not touching her. I reached out and covered her hand with mine. "You were right. I was using you as a way to cope. I wasn't giving you anything in return. I was obsessed with having you beside me. Knowing you were mine. That wasn't helping you. That was my trying to own you."

She didn't respond. But she didn't move her hand away either.

"We started this because you could listen and understand what I was dealing with when no one else could. Yes, you became my crutch. I wanted to be near you to draw from this amazing strength of yours."

She sniffled but didn't look back at me.

"Things changed, though. Yes, you became someone I

could lean on, but you also became more than that. I looked forward to hearing your voice, seeing your smile, and, God, listening to you laugh. I love the way you laugh. All of those things became things I loved. I would have never . . ." I stopped. What I needed to say I wanted to make sure I said right. I didn't want to screw it up. This was important. This was my chance to fix all I'd messed up.

"That night we . . . when we slept together. Maggie, I—" I needed her to look at me. Reaching over, I slid a finger under her chin and turned her face until her eyes met mine. "Maggie, I knew I loved you then. I didn't tell you because my emotions were so raw that night. I didn't make love to you because I needed comfort. I made love to you because I wanted to be as close to you as possible. Because, although I had lost my dad, I had been given you. Someone who made me feel whole inside. Who gave me a reason to smile every day. And I let myself go a little insane with my need to hold on to you. I don't want to possess you, Maggie. I want to belong to you. I'm willing to give you all the time you need. But you have to know I am in love with you." I dropped my finger from underneath her chin and moved my hand away from hers.

She didn't say anything as her wide eyes filled with tears. It took every ounce of willpower I could muster to leave her there and walk away.

CHAPTER 47

MAGGIE

He loved me.

Everything he said was more . . . It was what I needed.

The sadness and ache that had taken up permanent residence in my heart were lifted. West Ashby loved me. I wasn't just someone he needed to get through his loss. I was more than that.

"Wait," I called. He'd walked off behind me, and I turned around to see he'd only gotten halfway down the hall. He stopped, and for a second I wasn't sure he was going to look at me. When he finally did, his eyes held hope. So much hope I could see it from where I stood.

I called out to him again. "I didn't want you to wake up

one day and not need me anymore. I wouldn't have been able to survive that kind of heartbreak. I wanted more. I fell in love with you, and it terrified me."

He started walking back to me, his long strides determined as he kept his eyes locked on mine. When he reached me, he cupped my face in his hands and stared down at me. "Thank God," he said fiercely before his lips covered mine.

I clung to his shoulders as happy tears slid down my cheeks. His thumbs brushed them away as our tongues collided and we held on to each other as if it were the last time.

"You're not real good with the giving-her-space thing, are you?" Brady's voice startled me, and I pulled back and glanced over West's shoulder to see my cousin looking more amused than anything.

West grinned, then pressed a kiss to the tip of my nose before sliding his arm around me and turning to look at Brady. "Apparently not," he drawled as he smirked at my cousin.

Brady laughed and shook his head. "As long as she's happy," he replied. Then his gaze met mine. He was looking for an affirmation from me.

"I'm very happy," I assured him.

He nodded then moved his gaze back to West. "Show me that you deserve her."

West's arm tightened around me. "I will."

"Good. Because I can't go kick Raleigh's ass, but I can kick yours."

This time it was me who laughed.

Tonight I had a date with West. A real date. The kind a couple goes on. The kind we'd never really had before.

It was only slightly awkward when Uncle Boone asked West where we were going and reminded him to take good care of me. I think I preferred sneaking out of my window to that. West didn't seem bothered by it, though; he seemed pleased more than anything.

As we drove down the road, he patted the seat beside me. "Scoot over here."

I did as I was told and happily moved to sit as close to West as possible.

"You haven't asked where we're going," he said as he put his hand on my leg.

"Because I don't care as long as I'm with you."

He grinned and squeezed my thigh. "I know that feeling."

I laid my head on his shoulder. "So, tell me where we're going."

"Well, I had several ideas, but none of them seemed special enough for our official first date."

That didn't answer my question. Not that I really cared, but I was getting curious now. "That tells me nothing."

He chuckled. "No, I guess it doesn't."

He was teasing me. "Why do I feel like I got tricked into this conversation without knowing it?"

West kissed my head. "I've decided telling you doesn't make it sound as good as it actually is."

When he turned to head down a road that led to the field party, I sat up and watched. There weren't any field parties tonight. What was he doing?

"Are we going to the field?" I asked.

He didn't respond. A small grin tugged on his mouth, but that was all I got.

So I waited.

Sure enough, West pulled his truck into the empty clearing and cut the engine. He stared straight ahead for a moment then finally turned to me.

"It was here I saw you for the first time. I thought you were beautiful. Might as well know that. You had me with just one glance. But I had left my mom at home with my sick dad, and I was worried. I felt guilty because I was here. I was angry because I couldn't just be here and enjoy it. My dad was slipping away from me, and I was terrified." He paused and reached for my hand. "That night I was broken and close to shattering. The pain was becoming unbearable, and I had no one. . . . Then there was you."

I felt my eyes sting from unshed tears. Thinking over

the past month since the first time I'd met him, so much had happened. His pain may have been what had drawn us together, but I would take it away in a second if I could. Even if it meant not having this with him now.

"I took what I wanted that night. You were a distraction at first. You were this gorgeous, silent girl who hid in the shadows. I wanted to lose myself in you. And for a brief moment I did just that. The taste of your lips was sweeter than anything I'd ever experienced. For a second I forgot my pain. My fears. My anger. And I just enjoyed being with you." He picked up my hand and kissed my knuckles before turning it over and kissing my palm. "I had no idea how precious you were. No idea that I'd just found the one to stand by me, to hold on to me and to help me learn to heal. I'm so thankful you opened up to me and spoke. When I think about not having you, it hurts. I couldn't have faced what I've faced without you."

A tear slipped free, and West moved his hand to catch it with his finger. "You became the most important part of my life. I don't want you to ever question that. And I'd like to do-over the first night we met," he said with a grin.

Do-over?

"What?" I asked, confused, as he opened the truck door.

He stepped down then, turned around, and got my hand to pull me to him. "I want a do-over," he repeated, then winked at me. "In order to do this right, I need you to go stand over by that tree and look like your usual breathtaking self. Once you're in place, we are repeating the events of that night. But instead of me being hurt and angry, I'm going to be the guy you needed. The one you healed. I'm going to sweep you off your feet so fast, you won't know what hit you."

This time I laughed as another tear slipped free. I nodded and walked over to the tree where I had gotten my first kiss. That night I had been so lonely until West had shown up. He'd brightened my world, and he didn't even realize it. He thought he needed to do it over.

I disagreed. But I went along with it.

West gave me a thumbs-up when I was standing exactly where he'd seen me that first night. As he walked over just like he'd done then, I wanted to giggle. It seemed silly, but it was sweet. I'd give him that.

"Why are you out here all alone? The party's in there." He nodded toward the clearing in the woods.

I bit back my grin. "Am I supposed to talk or be silent? I wasn't talking back then," I said quietly, trying to keep a straight face.

West cocked an eyebrow at me and lowered his head until his lips were very close to mine. "You're not very good at do-overs, are you?" he asked me.

I giggled. "You didn't make that part clear!"

He kissed the corner of my mouth. "Let's just get to the good part. I excel at this scene," he whispered, then covered my mouth with his.

That first night I'd been so unsure. So much had changed since then. I knew exactly what to do now. I slid my hands up his arms, loving the way they flexed under my touch, before holding on to his shoulders.

Our tongues danced and teased while West's hands moved just under the bottom of my shirt and brushed against my skin. That definitely hadn't happened that night. But tonight I wanted it to. I lifted my hands higher and locked them around his neck, making my shirt rise and tempting West to touch more.

He did.

Both his hands moved up and cupped my breasts as a small cry that I couldn't help escaped me. I loved his hands on me and the way they made me feel.

Too suddenly he pulled back. "If I'd done this that night I would have expected you to knee me in the balls," he said, breathing hard.

"I probably would have fainted."

He kept his hands on me and brushed his thumb over my nipples through the satin of my bra. I shivered and squirmed, trying to get more.

"We aren't ready for this part of our night. I have a plan," he said, his eyes full of the same arousal I was feeling.

"I thought this was your plan," I said, closing my eyes as he moved his fingertips just inside the satin of my bra.

"No, but it is a helluva lot better."

Take All the Time You Need
CHAPTER 48

WEST

Two weeks later . . .

I held Maggie's hand as we stood at her mother's grave. Last night after the game we hadn't gone to the field to celebrate. Instead we'd packed our bags. Maggie hadn't been to her mother's grave since the funeral she barely remembered. When she'd shared that with me, I had wanted to get her there.

I visited my dad's grave every Saturday morning to tell him about the game the night before. It helped me cope. It made me feel like he was close even if he wasn't there. I wanted that for Maggie.

Her small hand slipped out of mine as she turned to look up at me. Brady was waiting in the truck for us. His being there was the only way her aunt and uncle would approve of an overnight trip.

"I want to talk to her alone," Maggie said softly.

I bent down and pressed a kiss to the corner of her mouth. "Take all the time you need." Then I turned and left her there to face her past and her pain. I wanted to hold her hand while she did it, but I wasn't going to force her. I just wanted to be there when she needed me.

Brady glanced over at me and frowned when I opened the passenger door. "You leave her there all alone?"

"She asked to be alone."

He sighed and picked up his phone and then handed it to me. "Just got this text from my dad. He didn't call because he was afraid Maggie would hear him. They want to tell her."

I read the text several times as my stomach twisted and my heart felt heavy.

Her father had hanged himself in his cell this morning. There were no details on how he'd managed to do that. Maggie acted as if he was already dead, but how would this affect her? I turned to look at her as she stood by her mother's grave.

She had faced so much that I hated adding more to it. I

wished I could keep this from her, but I knew she deserved to know. Seeing her hurt was hard.

"I called Dad. He said her dad left her a letter. Dad is going to get it and read it first. We don't know if she should see it. She just started talking and living life again."

"Don't tell her without me there," I told him.

"We won't," he replied.

One day we would look back at this time, and the pain wouldn't be so fresh. I wanted that day to get here.

I Cried for Me

CHAPTER 49

MAGGIE

I'd fallen asleep at some point on the drive home. My head was tucked against West, and his arm was around me. I could feel his fingers gently playing in my hair. He made me feel warm and safe. I'd needed that after visiting my mother.

I hadn't been prepared. Knowing her body was underground was one thing. Seeing the actual grave was another. West's hand in mine had given me the strength I needed to face it. Once I had been sure I wasn't about to fall to the ground in a sobbing mess, I'd let him go so I could talk to her.

I'd told her all about life with Uncle Boone, Aunt Coralee, and Brady. I'd started from the day I'd arrived, and I'd tried to tell her all the important things. Especially about West and his dad. When I'd finished, I'd realized West was right. Talking to her had made it feel as if she were close to me somehow.

"Dad's texting me. He wants to tell her tonight," Brady's voice said in a whisper.

Her, as in me? What were they talking about?

West tensed underneath me, and I stayed still, my eyes closed. "She needs a little time after seeing her mom today," he said so softly, I wondered if Brady could hear him.

Brady sighed. "I agree. I'll talk to Dad. Your mom's home again? Right? Didn't she come home last week?"

West's mom was home, but she was acting strange. I knew he was worried about her. She had left so abruptly after his father's death and had gone to stay with her own mother, leaving West to deal with things alone. It didn't seem like her at all. Now that she was back, she was acting odd. Forgetting things, burning food, sleeping half the day.

"Yeah, she's home," he replied. The worry in his voice was obvious. I wanted to hold him and promise him it would all be okay. But I couldn't do that because I didn't know for sure that it would be.

I waited to see if they said anything more about what my uncle wanted to tell me. When they didn't after several minutes, I stretched and slowly sat up.

"About time you woke up. You've slept most of the drive," Brady said in a teasing tone.

West chuckled and pulled me to him as he kissed the top of my head. "Leave my girl alone. She's had a long day."

West knew what my uncle Boone was going to tell me. If I asked him, he'd tell me. He wouldn't keep it from me. I tilted my head up to look at him. He tilted his head down to meet my gaze.

"Thank you," I said.

"Anything," he replied. He didn't have to say more, because I knew what he meant. He'd do anything I needed. Anything I asked of him.

"Can we stop it with the sweet shit, please? Y'all aren't alone," Brady said.

West smirked. I loved that smirk.

I waited until West went home to check on his mother before going downstairs to confront my uncle Boone. Brady and West knew something I needed to know, but they both wanted to protect me. As much as I appreciated that, I wanted to know what it was.

Uncle Boone was sitting in his recliner, a book in his hands. He looked up at me over his reading glasses. I saw a brief flicker of concern before he masked it and smiled at me.

"Did you have a good trip?" he asked.

"I needed that. To see her," I told him. "But I also need

to know what it is that Brady and West don't want me to know yet."

Uncle Boone frowned and then put his book down before taking off his glasses. "You've been through a lot today, Maggie."

I had. He was right. But that didn't change the fact I had a right to know this secret that affected me. "I want to know."

He motioned for me to sit down across from him on the sofa. I considered telling him I would just stand, but I walked over to the sofa and took a seat. He clearly didn't want to tell me whatever it was, and I knew it had to be something to do with my father.

I gripped my hands tightly in my lap and waited.

Uncle Boone studied me a moment before speaking. "It's your father . . . ," he began. The dread and fear that came with those few words sank in. "He's dead, Maggie. They found him this morning."

He's dead.

Two words that should mean sadness, devastation, pain, but that only gave me a sense of emptiness. I wanted to feel relief, but I couldn't. He'd taken my mother from me. Cut short her life and ruined everything. I wanted to cheer that he was gone. That I'd never see his face again.

But I couldn't.

Instead I just sat there, repeating those two words over
and over in my head. It was over. *He's dead.*

The good memories I had of him didn't outweigh the
bad. There were too many bad. Too many sad memories.
Too many regrets.

My mother had been a beautiful object he'd wanted to
own. In the end he had owned her, then thrown her away
as if she were nothing. She'd loved him. I had seen it in her
eyes and in the way she wanted to please him. Yet nothing
she did was ever good enough. She wasn't what he'd hoped
for, yet he hadn't been able to release her and let her live
her life. He had kept her only to destroy her in the end. To
destroy us all.

I always believed he loved me. I had moments where
he made me feel cherished and precious. I wondered if my
mother had had the same. If that was why she'd loved him
so much. But he hadn't been worthy of our love.

I had hated him. I had wished he were dead.

And now he was.

But there was only emptiness. A void inside me.

"Maggie, I know he was your father. No matter what—"

"No," I said, stopping Uncle Boone from saying more.
"No. He wasn't my father. He stopped being my father
the day he took my mother from me. Don't tell me you're
sorry for my loss. Don't say that it's okay for me to grieve

for him, because he's been dead to me for two years. This just finalizes it."

Uncle Boone didn't try to say more. I stood up and hurried back to my room. Where I could be alone. Where I wouldn't have to talk.

Aunt Coralee came and knocked on my door a few minutes later. I assured her I was okay and wanted to be alone and didn't want to talk about it.

She didn't argue with me.

An hour later my bedroom window slid open, and West stepped inside. His face was etched with worry and concern. I stared up at him from my spot on the bed where I was sitting with my knees folded under me. The hollowness where the pain should be shattered, and the first tears broke free.

He was on the bed, pulling me into his arms, before the sobbing started. While I was safely tucked against him, I cried for all I'd lost. All I'd never have. I cried for my mother and how tragically she'd died. I cried for West and his dad. And I cried for me.

Epilogue

WEST

It wasn't until we were sitting at Brady's, looking through old photo albums several weeks later, that I realized who she was.

It was the Christmas that Brady and I were in seventh grade. He'd had to go to Tennessee for his family's Christmas party, and he begged his mom to take me with him. I had been before and I knew how boring it was, but he was my best friend. So I went.

We always took our football and tossed it outside, even in the snow, while the party went on. The only time we went in with everyone was to eat. There weren't any other kids but a girl. I had seen her a few years ago, the last time I came to this thing, but I hadn't seen her this visit. Not that I was looking.

Brady had gone inside to help his dad, and I'd decided to explore the house. I didn't get far before I heard someone crying. I debated going inside the room, hoping whoever it was didn't notice me standing there in the doorway. But she lifted her head, and the prettiest green eyes I'd ever seen looked directly at me. Long dark hair framed her face. The pink-and-silver bedroom reminded me of something from a fairy tale. It fit her.

She sniffled and continued to look at me. I wasn't sure if she wanted me to leave her alone or to ask her if I could do something. My momma hadn't raised me to run off and leave a girl crying, so I'd walked over and sat down beside her.

"It can't be all that bad. It's Christmas," I said, hoping to lighten the mood. I didn't mention the fact she reminded me of a princess and I'd never seen one of those cry on television.

She sniffed again and wiped at her face. "It doesn't feel like it," she'd whispered back.

"What with all the Christmas music and the way this house is decked out with more decorations than the entire town of Lawton? How can it not feel like Christmas?"

The girl looked away from me. Her face remained sad.

"Not everything is what it seems. Not everyone is what they should be or appear to be."

How old was this girl? She talked like she was grown. But she didn't look any older than Brady and me. "One of your friends do you wrong?" I asked. I knew about girl drama. Happened at school all the time.

"I wish," she whispered, not looking back at me.

She wasn't a real open book. I was getting tired of trying to cheer her up, because I obviously sucked at it. "Whoever it is isn't worth your time if they're making you sad like this."

Finally she glanced back at me. "We don't always get to choose who we give our time to. We don't get to choose our parents, for example. And we don't get to make their decisions for them. So it's not that simple. He's my dad. I love him. I have to love him. But he hurts her. She tries so hard to make him happy, but he's always off with someone else. Like tonight. He's supposed to be here. He promised her he would be."

I didn't know what that felt like. My parents loved each other and I could never imagine my dad hurting my mom. But it sounded like this girl had a very different life. One I wasn't envious of. Even if her house was bigger than the church I went to on Sunday. It was even bigger than Gunner Lawton's house, and that was big.

"Then yeah, that sucks," I said, not knowing what else to say.

"Yeah, it does," had been her only response.

Brady had called my name then, and because I didn't know what to do or what to say, I left her there. When she'd come to eat, I couldn't make eye contact with her because I felt guilty for not being able to help her. And for knowing her secrets.

We were both in the photo that they'd taken that night. When I saw her little girl face, the memories came flooding back. I'd completely forgotten about that girl and what she'd told me. But that Christmas I remembered thanking God for my parents. I realized I'd been blessed with good ones.

"That was you," I said, looking at her as my heart broke for the little girl I wanted to go back and hold. She'd shared her secrets with a stupid boy who'd done nothing to make her feel better.

She frowned as if she didn't know what I was talking about, and then her eyes lit with understanding. "Oh my God. I forgot. . . . I was so upset that night. But it was just one of many nights I felt that way," she said as her fingertip gently brushed over my face in the photo.

"You were the only person I ever told that to. I regret that. Not telling anyone my secrets. I might have saved her if I had," she whispered, lost in her thoughts.

I pulled her against me. I wasn't going to let her dwell on her regrets. "You were a kid. We both were. Confused kids who didn't know the right answer to anything. He was your father. You loved him. Don't blame yourself for something you couldn't control."

Maggie laid her head on my shoulder and her hand on my chest. "Thank you," she whispered.

I kissed her head. "I love you."

"I love you too," she replied.

I had always been told my future was on the field and I could be somebody great. And I had wanted that. Until I found somebody who needed me. And I realized the only person I wanted to be great for was her.

Acknowledgments

Going back to high school Friday nights, football games, first loves, first heartbreaks, and, of course, field parties has been something I wanted to do since I closed the Vincent Boys series in 2012. The story of West and Maggie has been building in my head for a very long time. I'm thankful that I was given the chance to write it. I loved every minute of it.

A big thank-you to my editor, Sara Sargent. She put up with my intensity while writing this story. She listened to me, and I believe with her help, this book has become the best it can be. Also I want to mention Mara Anastas, Jodie Hockensmith, Carolyn Swerdloff, and the rest of the Simon Pulse team, for all their hard work in getting my books out there.

My agent, Jane Dystel. She's there for me when I'm having a hard time working on a story, when I need to vent, and even if I just need a recommendation on a good place to eat in New York City. I'm thankful to have her on my side.

When I started writing, I never imagined having a group of readers come together for the sole purpose of supporting me. Abbi's Army, led by Danielle Lagasse, humbles me and gives me a place of refuge. When I need my spirits lifted, these ladies are there. I love every one of you.

Natasha Tomic and Autumn Hull for beta reading my

books and helping me make each story better. Without them, I would be lost. I love you both.

Colleen Hoover and Jamie McGuire for always being there and understanding me in a way no one else can. These two know my biggest faults and love me anyway. They get me, and in this world it's hard to find someone who can relate to what you're dealing with.

Last but certainly not least: my family. Without their support, I wouldn't be here. My husband, Keith, makes sure I have my coffee and the kids are all taken care of when I need to lock myself away and meet a deadline. My three kids are so understanding, although once I walk out of that writing cave, they expect my full attention, and they get it. My parents, who have supported me all along. Even when I decided to write steamier stuff. My friends, who don't hate me when my writing is taking over. They are my ultimate support group, and I love them dearly.

My readers. I never expected to have so many of you. Thank you for reading my books. For loving them and telling others about them. Without you, I wouldn't be here. It's that simple.